"Everybody loses their breath when they first walk onto the veranda."

Instant recognition stiffened her spine and caused her heart to flutter, then shudder. That voice...deeper, darker, more compelling, it was the same one that painted compliments on her skin, whispered dirty, delightful suggestions against her lips. Calla felt her knees weaken and clenched her fists, telling herself she couldn't pass out, couldn't gasp or sway or act like a fool.

What was she supposed to do? Say?

Biting down hard on her lip, she half turned and, as casually as possible, slipped her Audrey Hepburn glasses onto her face, hoping the gesture would give her a couple of seconds to gather her composure. But how was it that her sexy bartender was standing on the terrace of Judah Reyes's luxury St. Croix house...

Unless...no! Unless he was the owner, the CEO...

No. Way.

Dear Reader,

Welcome to St. Croix!

Ten months ago, Calla West did the unthinkable—she let go. During one magical weekend in St. Croix, she fell into bed with a younger, oh-so-charming bartender, and walked away with zero regrets.

Now, she's back on the island, invited to bid on the commission to revamp Sol House, an iconic mansion. She's a little older, a lot wiser, and utterly focused on rebuilding her interior design career after a crushing betrayal. She's got no time for love—until she walks into her next project and sees *him*.

Judah Reyes. Her one-night stand, her new client. The new CEO and heir to a global lifestyle empire, Reyes Luxe. But rekindling their connection won't be easy. Not with a jealous ex, tabloid drama and the whole world watching.

This is a story about second chances, finding yourself and a love that asks you to choose yourself and it—bravely, wholly and without fear.

I hope you fall for Calla and Judah the way they fall for each other—again, and that you love reading it as much as I loved writing it.

Happy reading!

With my very warm wishes,

Joss

xxx

Instagram: @josswoodbooks
Facebook: @JossWoodAuthor
TikTok: @JossWoodbooks

FOR BUSINESS... OR PLEASURE

JOSS WOOD

Recycling programs for this product may not exist in your area.

ISBN-13: 978-1-335-47078-2

For Business…or Pleasure

For questions and comments about the quality of this book, please contact us at CustomerService@Harlequin.com.

Harlequin Enterprises ULC
22 Adelaide St. West, 41st Floor
Toronto, Ontario M5H 4E3, Canada
www.Harlequin.com

HarperCollins Publishers
Macken House, 39/40 Mayor Street Upper,
Dublin 1, D01 C9W8, Ireland
www.HarperCollins.com

Printed in U.S.A.

Joss Wood loves books, coffee, wine and traveling—especially to the wild places of Southern Africa and, well, anywhere. Joss is a mom to two young adults, and occasionally attempts to grow things, with very mixed (mostly bad) results. She and her husband are bossed around by two cats and a Great Dane that is the size of a small cow. After a career in sales, local economic development and business advocacy, Joss writes full-time from her home in KwaZulu-Natal, South Africa.

Books by Joss Wood

For Business...or Pleasure
is Joss Wood's debut title for Harlequin Romance.

Harlequin Presents

Cape Town Tycoons

The Nights She Spent with the CEO
The Baby Behind Their Marriage Merger

Scandals of the Le Roux Wedding

The Billionaire's One-Night Baby
The Powerful Boss She Craves
The Twin Secret She Must Reveal

Hired for the Billionaire's Secret Son
A Nine-Month Deal with Her Husband
Fast-Track Dating Deception

Visit the Author Profile page
at Harlequin.com for more titles.

PROLOGUE

Ten months ago...

WORKING IN THE intimate bar of St Croix's Reyes Luxe hotel, adjacent to its world-famous wellness centre, Judah Reyes placed a mojito in front of the woman sitting at a high table closest to the bar. Her eyes didn't leave her phone, and she didn't register the drink or his presence. He took in her lovely profile, her straight nose and stubborn chin, and frowned. Judging by her rigid back and pale face, he wasn't sure when she last took a full breath.

Her screen was in his line of sight, and he saw a masculine hand resting on the inside of a slim tanned thigh, the faint tan line on his finger suggesting a recently removed wedding ring. Pointed red fingernails held a glossy brochure for the Reyes Luxe wellness centre. Maroon and gold, it looked a little old-fashioned, and very uptight. When he reached Reyes Luxe's marketing department, he'd suggest a corporate rebrand of their marketing assets to something less jaw-breakingly boring.

Actually, he had a lot of thoughts about Reyes Luxe's branding, the message they were promoting and the overall direction of the company. But that was a fight for later.

'He's like a toddler who can't be left alone for a minute. What a bastard.'

Her voice sounded disembodied, almost robotic. He'd served enough drinks to enough people to realise she was seriously rattled. 'Are you staying at this hotel?' he asked.

It took a couple of seconds for his words to land. She looked up at him, her pine-green eyes moving from his face to her drink and back again. 'Oh, hi. Thanks for bringing my drink over.'

She lifted her drink, and sucked. In the low lights of the bar, her long tawny hair—thick waves tumbling down her back—shimmered. She was small, petite, almost delicate, but she didn't need height to command attention. Pretty, sure, but it was a diluted word. She was effortlessly lovely, and heat-drenched desire shot down his spine.

Yep, and that was what made women like her extremely dangerous.

'Yes, I'm staying here for a few days, I have business here.'

Judah nodded at her phone. 'That doesn't look like business,' he said.

'My ex and his new girlfriend are here to, once again, mess with my life,' she replied bitterly.

Judah winced. While his parents had been happily married—they got hitched before the big money started rolling in—he'd grown up in and was part of a world where love was often linked to a business plan. When big money was at stake, relationships were often carefully negotiated contracts—strategic, sleek, and PR friendly. Few people married for love or for forever. They often married for the photos, to become a power couple, to maximise and merge brands.

He'd seen too many people stand at an altar, hand in hand, all smiles and designer tailoring, saying 'I do,' when what they really meant was, 'This will look good in a press release.'

Yeah, marriage had never been on his wish list. Not because he didn't believe in love, but because the real kind—messy, mutual, unfiltered—probably didn't exist. Not for someone like him. Not when your last name was Reyes and came with dollar signs and expectations.

Looking for a reason to hang around, Judah pulled a kitchen towel from his waistband and wiped the already clean table.

'How long have you worked as a bartender?' she asked.

'Here, a couple of months,' he replied, straightening. After earning his MBA at LSE a few years back, his dad had tried to slot him straight into a high-paying, decision-making executive role at Reyes Luxe. Judah immediately slammed on the brakes. What the hell did he know about running a global empire? Titles meant nothing if you didn't understand what powered and influenced them. So he'd opted for the long route.

It had been his choice to work within every department across the Reyes Luxe line—and because there were a lot of departments across multiple companies in ten or so countries, he might have a handle on the business in, hell, twenty years or so. Currently, he was gaining practical experience working in the food and beverage department of their St Croix hotel, and moonlighting as a bartender, a job he actually enjoyed.

The bonus? Being back on the island. To him, St Croix was more than just palm trees, clear sea and luxury villas—it was childhood summers and salt in his blood. It was home, even if he didn't live here full-time anymore. Judah looked around the bar, saw that no one needed his attention, and took in her beachy, floral dress, which dipped low to reveal the edges of a sexy midnight blue bra. Up close, he noticed her carefully applied make-up and curled hair. 'Are you waiting for him?' He nodded at her phone, still showing the photograph.

She snorted. 'As if.' She ran a finger around the rim of her glass, eyes fixed on the swirl of liquid inside.

'Hair, make-up, pretty dress,' he pointed out.

'Why do men automatically assume we dress up to look good for them?' she asked. Right. Fair point and he was an arse for assuming otherwise.

'Sorry,' he said. 'That was an asinine comment.'

She nodded, her eyes locked on his. She sighed, and her shoulders slumped. 'But you're not completely wrong.' She lifted her chin, green eyes flashing. 'If I run into him, and I probably will, I want him to know I'm thriving.'

'Are you?' he asked, not convinced.

She lifted one shoulder in a jerky shrug.

'I'm working on it. But he caused me a lot of grief, so I'm as good as I can be.' She wrinkled her straight nose. 'Why am I telling you this?'

He'd worked as a bartender through college and learned how to tune in to the vibes from his customers. He sensed their mood and instinctively knew when to speak and when his customers needed silence. 'People tend to talk to bartenders,' he reminded her. 'We're part magician, part therapist, part friend. I'm Judah, by the way.'

'Calla.'

'Judging from your accent, I'm guessing you are from New York.'

'And you're British.'

He'd been educated in the UK, but his childhood had been split between his parents' homes in New York, London and the Far East. And St Croix. 'Why are both you and your ex on the island at the same time?'

'Jack and I are both bidding on an island-based project,' she replied. Her eyes flicked past him, toward the door. Judah turned, the back of his neck prickling.

Blond. Early forties, and fit in that over-polished, personal-trainer-on-speed-dial way. Judah recognised the type. Confident swagger, expensive watch, the kind of smug smile that announced that he was an entitled rich son-of-a-bitch. Judah hated him on sight. Not because he was unfamiliar—but because he was *too* familiar. Judah'd grown up with boys who became entitled men—cocky, privileged, relying on their instantly recognisable surnames and family money. He'd watched them slip and slide through life, dodging their commitments and responsibilities. And through his dad, he listened to stories about how their fathers charmed, schemed, manipulated and broke situations and people. Hell, he'd seen his father use money, power and influence to get a desired result.

He'd been, was still, terrified he might be tempted to lean into the unearned privileges that came with his instantly recognisable name. Call him stubborn or stupid, but Judah didn't want to be lumped into the same rotting heap of trust fund arrogance and entitlement. He refused to be another rich boy who'd earned nothing, who traded off his name, who'd had everything handed to him.

Screw that.

So yeah, his reaction to him was visceral. It was bone-deep irritation that rose like steam before reason could take hold. Right, it was definitely time for him to walk away.

'Enjoy your drink,' Judah said, pushing down his protective instincts. What was wrong with him? She was, at least, five years older than him, definitely in her mid-thirties, and she didn't want or need his protection. But something about her reminded him of a once glorious wilted rose whose petals were one breath from being blown away.

Judah slid behind the bar and positioned himself at the end, close to her table. He glanced at his watch and saw he was five minutes from the end of his shift. With luck, he wouldn't have to serve Mr Slick. Standing back, he smiled as the next shift's bartender slid behind the bar. He quietly greeted her and silently thanked her for coming in early. She could take over...

But, because his curiosity remained, he'd stand there, just for a few more minutes.

Calla was the first to speak, and when she did, her voice was stronger than he expected. 'Where's your latest conquest, Jack?'

His smarmy chuckle drifted over to Judah. 'She was tired after we...*after*.'

Judah gritted his teeth. *Prick.*

'I'm sure I know the answer to this question,' she said, her voice cool and even, 'but why are you here, in St Croix?'

Judah dropped his head to hide his smile, appreciating her tone and detachment. He hoped it was a verbal slap across Jack's smug, self-important face.

'Same reason as you, darling,' he drawled. 'Along with two other designers, I'm meeting with the owner of Reyes Luxe, hoping to secure the redesign for his island property.'

Sol House? *Hell, no!*

His voice scraped across Judah's nerves—too smooth, too rehearsed, nails dragging over a blackboard. 'I did warn him,' the man added, voice dropping into fake sympathy. 'I told him you weren't suitable and not experienced enough for a project like this. But Mr. Reyes insisted on seeing your work.'

Judah thought fast, recalling his father saying something about meeting interior designers to revamp Sol House, but he'd been rushing to be on time to make his shift and hadn't paid much attention. Judah didn't move, didn't speak, heat building behind his ribs. This jerk-off had no idea just how badly he'd overplayed his hand. He was far down the food chain at Reyes Luxe—his choice—so Judah rarely stuck his nose in his father's business. But Sol House had been his mum's personal property—a sanctuary filled with his best childhood memories, the one place where he could breathe easier and be wholly himself. There was no way he'd let that smug, Armani-clad jackass set foot in the only house he truly loved.

Yeah, *no*.

Not happening.

He tuned back in to their conversation. 'You've obviously forgotten I interned on a project for Mr Reyes years ago, before I made the crucial mistake of marrying and starting a business with you.'

'No, your biggest mistake was thinking you could leave without my permission.' His smile was slow, lacking humour and stolen off a snake. 'You had no right to walk away from me, from my name and from the life I gave you. No right to think you can operate in my world without me.'

Whoa, narcissistic much? Who the hell did this guy think he was?

'Why am I even sitting here listening to you?' she murmured, looking more fragile than she did before. Broken, a little lost. And her ex, the man who'd promised to love her, was enjoying every second of her pain and discomfort.

Calla picked up her phone and slid out of her chair. She swayed a little and gripped the edge of the round table, a rag doll about to collapse in on itself. There was no way he could leave her looking like that...

Thinking fast, Judah ducked into the bar's tiny stock room and pulled his black button-down shirt over his head, revealing a black, body hugging tank. He tugged it out of his black pants. Looking in the mirror behind the bar, he ruffled his slicked-back work-appropriate hair, and nodded when it fell over his forehead and into his eyes. He looked younger than he actually was, early twenties rather than late, ready to go bar hopping or clubbing, the tank showing off his muscled arms and chest.

It was time to put the good looks he'd inherited from his stunning mum to good use...

He shoved his wallet and phone into the pockets of his pants and ambled out from behind the bar, with what he hoped was a charming, anticipatory smile on his face. Walking straight up to Calla, and in one smooth move, he slid his arm around her too-thin waist and cupped her face in his hand. She was so warm, and she smelled like lime and lilies. Intoxicating.

He slid his hand to her lower back and tucked a long curl behind her ear, aiming to project a sense of familiarity, of shared intimacy. Calla opened her mouth to speak—the jackass looked both shocked and pissed off, and he didn't want her undoing all his good work—and he lowered his head to rest his lips on her ear. 'Let's give him some of his own medicine, huh?'

Pulling back, Judah handed her an easy grin. 'I've been looking for you. Are you ready to go, gorgeous?'

He held out his hand, not sure if she'd take it or slap him. He desperately hoped for the latter, because he might punch Mr Slick if he smirked.

She blinked, her eyes wide, and Judah found himself mentally begging her to take his hand, to walk out of the bar with him. Many seconds later, her fingers met his, and he gave her hand a reassuring squeeze. He hauled air into his lungs and, pulling her as close to him as possible, led her out of the bar and into the warm Caribbean night.

CHAPTER ONE

TEN MONTHS LATER, in her Reyes Luxe hotel room on St Croix, Calla tossed her bag onto the white linen–covered double bed and walked over to the huge window dominating the space. The hotel overlooked Teague Bay's sun-drenched beaches and swaying palm trees. She'd forgotten that St Croix was a slow, honeyed sigh of an island, emanating a casual charm that seeped under the skin. The sea shimmered—emerald and sapphire light dancing on every swell and dip, bold, brilliant and utterly unapologetic. The colonial façades of the buildings were faded just enough to be romantic, and the scent of salt air was everywhere. It instinctively made her want to relax, to be a cat stretching out in the sun.

The memories of long-ago warm nights and hotter glances rolled over her, and she tasted the tang of lime and his kisses on her lips, remembering a tanned masculine body moving over hers. Part of her longed to be stretched out on a beach blanket beside someone she had no business wanting but couldn't stay away from—whispering midnight confessions between intense kisses, while the ocean listened in, shameless and uninvited.

Calla rocked back on her heels, the pretty hotel room fading, giving way to the still sharp, golden memory of him. The bartender with the crooked smile and sexy voice. The younger man who'd made an outrageous suggestion, and then, with complete aplomb, knifed Jack—metaphorically, obviously—between the ribs by walking her into the night. Outside, instead of dropping her hand and walking away, he'd looked at her like she was ice cream on a steamy day and expected him to suggest they find a bedroom. But that hadn't happened.

Not then anyway.

He'd simply held her hand—hers small and cool, his much larger and tanned—and led her down a stretch of moonlit sand. The surf bubbled over the sand, a crab dodged the waves and his voice soothed her as he told her stories of island lore, of rebels and pirates and forgotten kings. It was absurd and magical—and somehow he managed to push the tense run-in with her ex, the one who'd left a decade's worth of scars, far, far away.

And then, when the glow of bars and restaurants gave way to darkness, he'd stopped and cupped her face, holding her like she was something precious. Without hesitation, he'd lowered his head and kissed her, slow and deep and thorough, as if he had all the time in the world.

Later, he'd walked her to his motorbike, no helmet, no hurry, and driven her across the island, showing her his personal playground. She pressed her face to his back, hair flying, arms wrapped tight around his wide chest or ribbed stomach, feeling alive in a way she hadn't in years. Calla knew he kept driving long after they should've stopped, just because she said she loved the wind and the rhythm of the engine. She hadn't been brave enough to tell him she'd, most of all, loved feeling him between her legs.

Later, when the rising sun kissed the sea good morning, they finally tumbled onto the bed in that one-room, ramshackle surf shack by the sea where he loved her like he meant it.

Again. And again. And again.

The sex had been, was still, the best of her life. It was also the only sex she'd had since her divorce. Calla placed a hand on her stomach, aching for that magical time when time stood still. Where was he now? Was he still running free, kissed by the sea and the sun? Still smiling like a man with no weight on his shoulders?

She glanced at herself in the ornate mirror across the room, the antithesis of that beachy woman whom he'd loved so well. Her curly hair was ruthlessly pulled back, sleek and straight. Her make-up was flawless, her outfit impeccable. She exuded control, professional distance.

Beneath her polished exterior, she saw faint lines at the corners of her eyes, a tiny strand of silver near her temple. Her neck ached, and the tightness in it, and her shoulders never really went away. She worked harder for everything now—her body, her business, her sanity. That woman on the beach? Barefoot, windblown, laughing in the dark? Calla barely recognised her. In some ways, she was as much a stranger to that version of herself as she was to that gorgeous man she'd spent too little time with.

Calla shook her head and mentally snapped herself back to the now. She wasn't here to daydream or for a vacation, she was here to work. To take another shot at a once-in-a-blue-moon project, a commission that would supercharge her business, boost her career and hopefully, rehabilitate her reputation. Or at the very least, restore it to what it was before.

She couldn't afford to waste time or be distracted by St Croix's loveliness or by remembering that sexy deep-voiced bartender who'd made her body sing, and her soul sigh. She might be at a honeymooner's dream destination, but her focus would be, as it always was, on her work.

On landing the commission to redecorate and update Sol House. Calla kicked off her heels, opened the button on her fitted jacket, feeling the pull of her tight pencil skirt. She considered changing into a pair of cotton shorts and a T-shirt, but since she was due at Sol House in fifteen minutes, it wasn't worth the hassle.

After snatching a bottle of water from the bar fridge, she sat down on the bed and picked up her phone. As soon as she connected to the Wi-Fi, her phone started beeping with text and email notifications. Some from her assistant, one from her ex-husband.

She opened it and skimmed his words.

I hear you are in St Croix, and that you've been given an opportunity to submit a proposal to revamp Sol House. The project was abruptly put on hold last year, then shelved. Why are you getting the first crack at the commission?

She really should've deleted Jack's number months ago. Every time his name popped up on her screen—usually late at night, usually loaded with just enough nastiness to make her stomach twist—she thought, *Enough now. Cut him loose. I'm done.*

But she never hit that delete button.

Yes, she knew she was being perverse, and

that she was clinging to the thin whispers of what remained of a toxic relationship. She didn't miss him, *God. No.* She kept reading his messages because those smug, casual, caustic, acidic messages—interspersed with demands she return to work for him at Atelier Abernathy—reminded her of how he'd ripped her apart with a smile on his face. Jack was the vehicle by which she'd learned a dozen lessons, both big and small, all of them hard. He'd taught her how not to trust, about the cost in giving too much, believing too easily, loving too deeply. He was the reason she didn't let people in.

One moment, she'd been a rising star in New York's competitive interior design scene; the next, an outsider and a liability. Thanks to Jack and his influential family, her work dried up, and clients stopped returning her calls, and the truth settled into her bones: if you didn't protect yourself, no one else would. Love wasn't a partnership; it was playing Russian roulette.

So, no. She didn't delete his number. Because every time his name flashed across her screen, it reminded her why she had rules now. Why she kept her emotions locked down, her life airtight, her business above reproach. Why she never let herself lean. Never on clients. Not on colleagues. Not on lovers.

And especially not on men.

But Jack, as always, had impressive connections and somehow had learned that the managing director of the Reyes Luxe wellness brand wanted to know whether she'd be interested in revamping Sol House, his impressive mansion on the east shore.

She should've felt flattered. Proud, even. But instead, the offer made her suspicious. Like Jack, she was curious why she was the first designer through the door. After the past few years of hell—a toxic divorce, public embarrassment, a stalled career, clients ghosting her—she couldn't work out why she was here. On merit? She doubted it. Jack had torched her reputation as a rising-star interior decorator, especially among those who awarded the kinds of commissions that attracted attention and built careers.

And, dammit, she couldn't rid herself of the persistent, insistent voice whispering that she wasn't quite good enough. That she didn't belong in Jack's world of elite and old-money properties and projects. She tried to fight her inner critic, but it was exhausting. But, bottom line, she *needed* this job. Not only for her career, but to prove to herself that she could still create. That her work still mattered. That *she* mattered.

Calla sighed, squared her shoulders and took a breath. Obsessing over the past wouldn't get the job done. Whatever the reason, being the first one in the door was a hell of a coup for a small designer operating a lean, independent studio out of a shared space in Brooklyn. While her name was, she hoped, quietly gaining traction again, she wasn't an A-list designer anymore, someone the owner of Reyes Luxe would normally contact. Maybe, because he was British, he wasn't au fait with what was happening in the NYC design scene and hadn't heard about her fall from grace.

But, because the email hinted at future work with Reyes Luxe if she satisfied the owner's expectations, she wasn't going to look a gift horse in the mouth. Or a commission that would give her immediate legitimacy, her career a life-changing boost. It was a lifeline, a high-profile, international contract that had the power to reset her entire reputation—under her own name, on her own terms.

Of course, she was going to take a shot at it. She wasn't an idiot. Or, to be scrupulously fair, she wasn't an idiot *anymore*.

According to his board of directors, his CFO and upper management, and his two assistants, there were a thousand things Judah Reyes should've been doing—in London, Singapore and New York. Instead, he stood barefoot on the veranda of Sol House, hands in the pockets of his chino shorts, staring at the horizon like it held the answers.

The sun was hot on his back, burning through his cotton button-down and making his skin prickle. The sea, far below him, rolled up onto the small private beach bordered by rocks, quietly relentless. Judah stretched and yawned. He'd had a fitful few hours of sleep and couldn't remember the last time he'd slept through the night. Definitely not since his father died, collapsing in the middle of a board meeting last year. One moment a titan, the next he was gone. His death had been the event that split life into before and after, a mental rift in Judah's psyche.

Judah before had been laid-back, happy to work behind the scenes and to be underestimated, perfectly content with taking his time to learn the family business, knowing that he had years, *decades*, before he needed to step into his father's too-large, too charismatic shoes. He'd been learning the business, taking his time, preferring to prioritise having a work-life balance rather than working the consistently long hours his father did. Though, looking back, it was fair to say that the work-life balance had been tilted toward having fun—working a little, surfing, travelling and partying more. His dad—larger than life, self-made, soft with Judah in a way he wasn't with the world—had encouraged it. *Take your time, son. There's no rush.*

He'd lied.

Instead of running the company for the next ten, twenty years, David succumbed to a massive heart attack and handed Judah a legacy, an international company and a harsh spotlight. He'd stepped up because he had no choice, not because he felt ready. And ten months on, he still didn't. He'd become a master of keeping his expression neutral as he signed off on multimillion-dollar deals, but under his tie and suit, his throat was tight and his heart careered off his ribcage as he second-guessed every decision. Would he ever feel like he belonged at the helm of Reyes Luxe? Would his father approve of and be proud of the job he was doing?

Out of the office, he smiled for the cameras on red carpets and magazine covers, but he didn't recognise the man wearing his face dressed in Thom Browne and Zegna suits, hair carefully styled.

St Croix and Sol House were the only places he could still breathe—just a little. Sol House held most of his memories of his mum, and was the only one of his properties that felt real, where he could remember his father as being just a dad. The house still smelled like his dad's cigars and sun-dried linen. This was where his father taught him to swim, to paddle, to surf. Where they sailed and swam and talked about everything and nothing. After his mum passed, and for a month every summer, they'd spent time here, just the two of them. He hadn't been back since his death, and the house felt lifeless, cold, abandoned, filled with silence and the echoes of happier times.

The sea beckoned him to come play, but he'd yet to walk down the path to the secluded cove. He'd arrived the day before yesterday, and all he'd done was work. He put his foot down this morning, telling his assistant he didn't want to be disturbed unless the markets crashed or aliens landed. The reality was that he might have today, Friday, and this upcoming weekend to himself. If he was lucky.

Judah pushed his hand through his hair and released a frustrated sigh. He also needed to figure out where to take the company, what he wanted from it. He'd just finalised his dad's last planned project and from now on, the direction of Reyes Luxe was his alone—every win, every loss, every person's job, share prices, returns and dividends were on him.

It felt...heavy. Overwhelming.

After his father's death, he'd avoided St Croix and the house, telling himself he was too busy to visit. And he had been, initially, he'd barely had time to breathe. But as the shock faded, he started questioning everything—where he was going, what the company stood for, who he was, what he wanted—and he started craving silence and salt water. The urge to feel like himself, not the face of Reyes Luxe, burned through him and threatened to consume him. He craved authenticity and to reconnect with who he was before…before he became an icon, an heir, a brand. But that version of himself—unguarded, unpolished, whole—felt like a stranger he couldn't quite reach.

The last time he truly felt like himself was ten months ago, right here in St Croix—a few days before his dad died, when he was laughing with and loving Calla. It was the last time he'd felt fully relaxed, completely at ease in his skin. Lately, for some strange, irrational reason, he couldn't shake the feeling that being with her again might help him find that version of himself. It was bizarre. Nuts. But the thought lingered. Then it hit him—Calla was a designer, and the only reason she'd come to the island in the first place last year was to pitch for the Sol House renovation.

Sure, the house needed upgrading, but it was low on his priorities and, truthfully, it was an excellent excuse to see Calla again. So he'd told his assistant to make her an offer to be the first person to submit her designs for the revamp. He wasn't committing to anything just yet; depending on whether he liked her ideas, he might hire her.

And she was arriving—he glanced at his Breitling—shortly. His breath caught in his throat, and his heart rate accelerated. He didn't believe in lasting connections and relationships were too risky. He'd lost his father between one heartbeat and two. Love was just another way to be gutted by grief. And really, no one was able to see him beneath the gloss and money. But Sol House held the version of him he missed, the man who didn't carry the weight of a billion-dollar empire on his back. And during those thirty-six hours with Calla, he'd been the best version of himself—unfiltered, open and fully alive.

And maybe—if he was lucky—these next few weeks with Calla would show him the way back to being the man he used to be.

Sol House stood behind a private gate on St Croix's northeast shore and was exactly as Calla had expected—elegant, expansive and quietly breathtaking. Calla stepped through the columned entrance, past the murmuring fountain and into the great room, where crystal chandeliers caught the Caribbean light like diamond drops. The bones of the house were beautiful—vaulted ceilings, French doors, curated art she'd presumed would be kept—but the interior was stuck somewhere between the '80s and death.

She remembered the photos she'd been sent by the CEO's PA: the kitchen was a black granite shrine, the heavy old-fashioned dining table sat twelve, and the bedrooms? Bland and boring and in desperate need of charm and soul. The east wing was all size and shine—spa baths, gold-veined marble, walk-in closets—while the master suite within the west wing boasted a lounge, terrace and more bland and boring. The library cum office, separating the master bedroom and lounge, was a gem, with soft light and comfortable furniture, and an exceptional view, all perfect for daydreaming.

Despite its mishmash styling, the house was a love letter to old-style Caribbean living. Just a little worn, a little faded. The design brief she'd received from his PA—if it could be called that!—was to make it sophisticated enough for upscale entertainment, but it still had to feel like a home. Sure. *Easy.* She'd solve the Middle East crisis while she was at it.

Calla's heels click-clacked on the Italian marble as she crossed the great room, walking behind a casually dressed woman who introduced herself as Bella, the part-time housekeeper. She wanted to stop and inspect what she thought might be a Jim Lambie on the wall, a Nicholas Hlobo sculpture in the far corner. Reminding herself that she would be spending the next two weeks—at least!—in this house and on the island, and to be patient, she checked that the zip of her pencil skirt was in the middle of her back, and the pendant of her necklace rested in the centre of her throat. Yes, she was detail oriented, but in her job, she had to be.

Details, control and self-reliance, along with independence, were the four cornerstones of her life.

Her thoughts stopped as she caught sight of the view off the expansive balcony. Calla placed her hand on her heart and simply stared, her lungs forgetting how to haul in air. The ocean was so endless, compelling, and an indescribable shade of blue, not turquoise or sea-green or aqua, simply undefinable and delightful. Sea and so much of it. She glanced at the blue infinity pool extending a little way off the cliff and easily imagined her arms on the edge, feeling she was about to fall into the sky and sea.

She'd admired houses before—even coveted a few—but she'd never fallen head over heels for one. Not like this, and not until now. The view was *everything*. The kind of everything that made her brain misfire and her heart stutter.

'Everybody loses their breath when they first walk onto the veranda.'

Instant recognition stiffened her spine and caused her heart to flutter, then shudder. That voice…deeper, darker, more compelling—it was the same one that painted compliments on her skin, whispered dirty, delightful suggestions against her lips and called her name when his orgasm rushed over him. Calla felt her knees weaken and clenched her fists, telling herself she couldn't pass out, couldn't gasp or sway or act like a fool.

Couldn't…*holy hell.* What was she supposed to do? Say?

Biting down hard on her lip, she half turned and, as casually as possible, slipped her Audrey Hepburn glasses onto her face, hoping the gesture would give her a couple of seconds to gather her composure. But how was it that her sexy bartender was standing on the terrace of Judah Reyes's luxury St Croix house…

Unless…no! Unless he was the owner, the CEO…

No. Way.

Way.

Calla resisted the urge to bite her lip as she took him in. He looked taller, bigger, meaner… older. His shoulders were as wide as she remembered, his chest as broad. The face she remembered had been open and ready to smile, but now his expression held shadows. His lips were thinner and pressed together. She couldn't see a hint of his dimple, and his eyes were darker, flatter, lacking the warmth from before. This was, but wasn't, the same person.

'It's been a while, Calla. Have you been well?'

He sounded like he was ordering coffee, like they'd met last week, like he hadn't buried his head between her legs, making her crash and burn, like he hadn't made her laugh. Or think. Or wish she could give up her New York life to live in a one-room surf shack beside the sea.

'What? I don't understand—'

He lifted one bigger shoulder. 'It's pretty simple, really. Last year, my father wanted this place revamped and invited three or four designers to submit designs, yours being one of them. The following week, he died of a heart attack.'

Calla grimaced. 'I heard that. I'm sorry for your loss,' she murmured. She'd received a generic email from someone last year informing the designers of his death and that the project to revamp Sol House had been shelved.

He nodded briefly. 'Sol House needed revamping then—it needs it more now.'

Okay, she understood that much. 'Your PA told me I'm the only one who's been asked to submit designs to upgrade your home. I don't understand why you haven't asked other designers to pitch their proposals, as well.'

He hesitated, an action so brief that Calla wasn't sure if she'd imagined it or not. 'I'm trying to take a vacation, and I didn't want a gaggle of designers invading my space, so I thought I'd start with you,' he told her.

His reply made sense, but… Calla tilted her head, trying to read the flicker in his eyes. What did it signify—challenge? Regret? Something else entirely?

'If I like what you do,' he continued, smooth as glass, 'it could lead to more work with Reyes Luxe. A few of my wellness centres, including the one here on St Croix, are due for a refurbishment.'

Damn, that was one hell of a carrot. For a small designer, landing Sol House would be impressive, working on a Reyes Luxe property would be career defining. His name on her portfolio would put her on the map in all the right ways. It would also shut Jack the hell up. That would be a huge bonus.

But something still tugged at her gut. The offer was golden, yes—but why did it feel like there was more beneath the surface than what he was saying? Like he wasn't just handing her an opportunity but also daring her to take it.

Like his offer was the tip of a massive, concealed iceberg?

Her mind reeled, trying to make sense of the past few minutes. 'Sorry, you've caught me off guard. I thought you were a bartender, a surfer, not the CEO and owner of one of the world's most recognisable brands.' Over the past few months she'd been too busy keeping her head down and working herself to the bone to stay afloat to pay much attention to the news, business or otherwise.

His eyes darkened, and his lips thinned. 'When we met, I was a bartender, I did surf, all the time, and I wasn't in charge. That all happened after…' He pushed his hand into his hair. 'After.'

His frown didn't lift. Stepping closer to her, Judah used his finger and thumb to pull her sunglasses off her face. Well, there was no hiding now. His eyes darted across her face, and wherever they landed, she felt their impact, a tingle, a buzz. Her cheeks reddened as she remembered him looking at her like this just before he…

Okay, can't think about that now, he was her client. Her very rich, very influential, very sexy client. Dear God, she'd slept with her client. Potential client…*whatever.*

'I prefer your hair curly, and you wearing a loose dress and being barefoot,' he said, handing her her glasses. Their fingers brushed, and sparks skittered up her arm, into her core.

Oh no! No! No! No! She still couldn't be attracted to him. That wasn't, on any planet or in any galaxy, acceptable.

She knew where that road led. Mixing business and romance had already blown up, rather spectacularly, in her face. Jack had made sure of that. She'd trusted him with her heart, her future, her career—and when he was done with her, he'd dismantled all three with the efficiency of a nuclear strike.

She'd been left with a crater where her confidence used to be.

So no, she couldn't go down that road again. She was in a never-ending battle to restore her professional credibility. She couldn't risk the progress she'd made for a man who made her stomach flip every time he smiled. The human equivalent of—she glanced at the ocean beyond his big bicep—that yacht skimming out to sea and disappearing from view.

Attraction was dangerous. And trust wasn't something she believed in anymore. Calla swallowed and gripped the handle of her tote bag tightly. 'I came dressed for a business meeting, to meet a potential client.'

Not you.

'It's good to see you again.' If it was, why had

he never bothered to track her down before this? It wouldn't have been hard to do. Calla pushed that thought away, annoyed with herself. She knew very well that a one-night stand was all he'd offered, and that any further conversation or connection hadn't been part of the deal.

Besides, she'd been a mess last year and would've been horrified if Judah rocked up in Brooklyn, looking to reconnect. She hadn't had the mental capacity back then—didn't have it now—to pay attention to anything but work, to rebuilding her name and her company. He would've been an unwanted and unwelcome distraction.

So why was she disappointed? Stupid. And illogical.

Judah pushed his hand through his too-long hair, and the ends brushed the collar of his cotton shirt. Then he gestured to the chairs sitting under the roof of the veranda. 'Let's get out of the sun,' he suggested. He looked at the lady who let her in, and Calla caught a small smile on his lips. 'Bella, could you bring us something to drink?' He turned to Calla, his eyes connecting with hers. 'Freshly squeezed juice, iced tea or water?' he asked.

How could he ask her about liquid refreshments when her brain had been deep fried? She forced herself to concentrate. 'Anything is fine.'

Judah ordered iced tea and gestured for her to take a seat. Calla placed her bag and portfolio case on the seat beside her and licked her lips. What was the protocol when your potential client also happened to be the hottest mistake of your life? Or maybe not a mistake—just a memory you'd replayed too many times, always in the dark, always alone.

Calla decided to bite the bullet. 'What's this all about, Judah?'

He took a moment to answer her. 'Last year, you—and one or two other designers who probably didn't hear about my father's death—sent in your renovation plans for this house, just like my father requested.' When Judah slipped into that formal tone, Calla could picture him in a sharp suit, behind a massive desk at Reyes Luxe, running the show. 'I've finished the business projects he started before he died—I'd like to finish this personal one too. So I looked at those designs.'

Calla waited for him to say something about her work, to compliment her designs, but he just looked at her, silent and sombre. He wasn't the carefree man she'd spent the night with, the one who complimented her easily and frequently. He was her client, and this was a professional situation.

It would've been a lot easier to get her head

around that concept if she could stop replaying the way he'd lifted her like she weighed nothing, holding her steady against him as he kissed her absolutely senseless. She shook her head, trying to concentrate on the here and now, but, behind her eyelids, images of him whipping off his shirt, acres of tanned skin exposed to her touch, flickered, then burned. The way he looked at her, with reverence and appreciation as he undid the clasp of her bra, his fingertips sliding over her nip—

Work, Calla! You are here as a professional decorator, not as his one-time, brief lover. That was in the past...way in the past.

Calla wiggled in her chair, grateful when Bella placed a glass in front of her. She thanked her, lifted it to her lips and sighed at the combination of mint, lemon and ice. She drained half and leaned back in her seat, and tucked her foot behind her calf. It was time to stop remembering and start business-ing. *Compartmentalise, Calla. You're good at that.*

'Something about what I did back then must've resonated with you for you to invite me back.'

He didn't drop his eyes from hers and, once again, she felt like she was missing out on a fairly significant puzzle piece. Something that would bring the picture into focus.

'Is that what happened?' she pressed.

He took a long time to answer her. ‘Something like that,’ he said, not giving anything away.

Calla didn’t believe him.

CHAPTER TWO

JUDAH RAN A hand through his hair and stared out over the infinity pool, where the horizon blurred the edge of the Caribbean sky and sea. He'd done the right thing by bringing Calla here. The second he saw her standing in the foyer—tote bag in one hand, proficiency wrapped tight around her like armour—he'd known.

Calla was the only choice. Professionally, sure. But also…inexplicably, personally. It didn't make any sense—it was something that no one would understand…it simply was.

He allowed his eyes to wander over her, taking in what remained the same, the changes. She was older, but then, so was he. This Calla was sleeker, sharper, spikier. Harder. But he'd caught something familiar in her eyes, the flash of curiosity, the spark of excitement as she took in his dated, but still glorious house. She stirred something in him he hadn't felt in a long time. Something reckless. Something real.

The moment her fingers brushed his, when

their eyes first connected and he inhaled her light perfume, he experienced an unfamiliar pulse in his veins, something he hadn't felt since…well, *her*. It was need, and want, the thrill of taking a risk. The time they spent together was a looping movie playing on his mind's big screen—highlighting her laughter, her unfiltered honesty, the occasional flashes of vulnerability and insecurity she probably thought she hid. He still remembered the creamy heat of her skin, the salt on her lips, them sharing stories like they had all the time in the world, their out-of-control passion.

But he never expected her to *still* affect him as much as she did.

Judah exhaled and rubbed the back of his neck. She hadn't known who he was then. She'd simply seen him. Just him.

No one had—not truly—for almost a year now. But a small part of him, the piece that still clung to ideas like fate and magic, couldn't help but wonder if he'd been…God, he mocked himself for even thinking it…*guided* to bring her back into his life. He recalled how he felt, just a month ago, flat and uninspired, burdened, while he unenthusiastically searched for an old set of plans on his dad's laptop. The folder labelled *Sol House Revamp* on the system jumped out at him and curiosity got the better of him. He clicked—

and there it was. Her name. Another impatient click later, and he was staring at her work.

He'd scanned her proposal, then went back for another, deeper, look. While he hadn't loved everything about her submission, it was immediately obvious she understood the soul of his house. Its wear, its warmth, its history. Its wounds. The other designers had seen a luxury property, but she'd seen a home.

Her vision, back then, wasn't about making Sol House something it wasn't, and her proposal centred around bringing it back to life. Then he started wondering about what it would be like to be with her at Sol House, watching her work on ideas for revamping the house. The idea of bringing her to St Croix had taken root and refused to be dislodged.

He told himself Sol House needed someone like her—a designer with sensitivity and restraint. That he needed to be there to answer her questions, to oversee things. But deep down, he knew the renovation wasn't the real reason he'd reached out. If he was being honest—truly honest—he was looking for something in himself. Chasing a version of the man he used to be, the one he'd last been with her: barefoot, sun-kissed, free. A man he could barely even remember.

He hadn't brought Calla here just to restore Sol House.

Admitting that to himself was hard enough. Telling her? Impossible. Not now. Maybe not ever. So he'd keep it professional and keep their attention focused on the project. Whatever was going on in his head, it was his to carry. He wouldn't lay the weight of his issues on her—or anyone.

He drained his glass of tea and crunched through an ice cube, lightly banging the base of his glass against his thigh. 'Sol House hasn't been updated since God knows when, and it desperately needs work.'

Calla tipped her head to the side and he was grateful when she didn't rush in to agree with him. This house was like a sibling; he could criticise it, but didn't like others doing the same.

'It's huge and every room needs an upgrade of one sort or another. Have you tackled a project this big?'

Calla rocked her hand up and down. 'Not a house, but I was involved in the renovation of a historic inn, which isn't that different. But big or small, my process is still the same.'

'Which is?'

'Nailing my client's vision, understanding his or her lifestyle, and wants and needs. Obviously, that would require us to sit down for a detailed briefing.'

Judah shifted, tension creeping into his shoulders. 'Can't we just walk through the house and call it good?' he muttered, his tone sharper than he intended.

It wasn't about curtains or couches. It was about *her*. About being here with her—*in this house, on this island*—and being bombarded by memories. Of his dad and his childhood. Of him and Calla together. Of the person he used to be.

Bringing Calla here had been great in theory, but it suddenly felt like too much. Like she might see too much. He'd brought her here to help him reconnect with the parts of himself he'd buried—but being this close to her was more challenging than he'd expected.

Calla crossed one leg over the other and rested her forearm on her knee. 'You're assuming that I'm going to take on your project, Judah. I'm not sure I am.'

Judah was fully aware of the power of the Reyes Luxe name, and he frequently used it as a carrot and a stick in business negotiations. He knew that if this project went out to tender, he'd have the best designers chomping for the chance to revamp Sol House, for a foot in the Reyes Luxe door.

He might be in St Croix, in casual clothes, but

this was just another negotiation—he was simply doing another deal. Yeah, and the sea below them was made of whiskey. He schooled his features and kept his expression imperturbable.

'Everyone in the industry knows that whoever lands the contract to design my house has a serious edge when it comes to future design work for Reyes Luxe—because they've already managed to impress me on a personal level. There's so much work that it would be a full-time position.'

Back then, she'd pleased him on an ultra-personal level, but he couldn't think about that now. Sure, inviting Calla here wasn't purely a business decision, but it wasn't fully personal either. He liked her designs, liked her work and thought she might be a designer he could work with. But she was also the woman he'd never been able to forget—the one who'd appeared shortly before he'd faced a major crossroads in his life, making him wonder if Fate was just messing with his head. But she didn't need to know any of that.

'You'd be a fool to turn down one hell of an opportunity because we slept together, Calla,' he said, keeping his tone bland.

'I'm not even sure I want to work for anyone or be a corporate designer, Judah,' she shot back. 'I like being my own boss.'

He respected that, and he also liked calling

the shots. It might be stressful and lonely, and he might second-guess himself daily, but now that he was used to power, he couldn't imagine giving it up or taking orders from someone else. The only difference between what he and Calla did was the amount of money involved and the scale.

'But what you can't deny is that your being here, after being asked to submit a proposal, is bound to get people talking. Right now, they are wondering what I know that they don't, whether they missed out on something special by not hiring you, and whether you are going to be the next big thing. If I like your proposal and hire you, you will be on everyone's lips, and the offers with roll in. The PR and publicity factor will be considerable. That's the power of Reyes Luxe, Calla.'

'When you put it like that...' she murmured, running her fingers across her forehead, the unconscious action suggesting she had a headache. He wasn't surprised since her hair was tight against her head and her clothes were more suited to corporate boardrooms. He looked down at her feet scrunched into tight two-inch heels and winced. She needed the wind in her hair and her toes in the sand...

And there he went, crossing the line from professional to personal.

'You're right—it's not an offer I can walk away from,' she said, sounding glum.

'I'm not leading you to an execution, Calla.'

She raised her eyes to look at his and cocked her head. 'No, of course you're not. So why do I get the feeling there's a lot more to this offer than what you're letting on?'

He knew what she was asking, whether he expected them to roll back the months to when he last saw her, naked and lovely in his bed. Whether that was part of the deal he was offering. Annoyance bit, but he forced it away. He couldn't blame her for thinking that way…

For centuries, millennia, men used their power over women to get their way, and the power balance was often tipped in their favour. He might've been a surfing bartender last year, but now he had the power and influence to change her life for the better. And she wanted to know what he wanted in return.

It was a completely fair question. But if he told her the truth—*please help me reconnect to who I was, take me back to a simpler time, hell, rewind time for me*—she'd run a mile. All he could do was reassure her that he expected nothing from her that wasn't work and design related.

What he hoped for was another story. 'You're here to do a job, to suggest a new look, to convince me it's what I want. I'm not going to pressurise you for more. It'll be strictly business for as long as you want it to be.'

Her head jerked up, and her gaze smashed into his. 'What does that even mean?'

'Exactly that. Nothing more. Nothing less.' Judah rose to his feet and slipped his hands into the pockets of his shorts. 'Spend the next few hours exploring the house, getting a sense of the scale of the project. Then come and find me and I'll take you on a tour of the grounds. Later this afternoon, you can give me your impressions and broad ideas for how you think it should be updated. If I like what you have to say, we'll move on to the next step.'

Well, on the plus side, she wasn't bolting for the door. Calla nodded and unfolded her long legs to push her way to her feet. 'Is there any room you'd prefer I didn't see at this point? A private place?'

He swallowed his snort. 'You've seen me naked, so seeing my bedroom or bathroom isn't that big a deal.'

She flushed, heat crawling into her cheeks, and he silently cursed. *Not helpful, Reyes. Professional, remember?* He looked down and frowned at her squished feet in her black heels, and just like that, made a new rule. 'Also, I'm not a fan of shoes in my house, so I'd prefer you remove yours.'

Because, damn, her feet needed a break.

Calla looked adorably confused as she removed one shoe, then the other, her head now not even reaching his shoulder. He'd forgotten how petite she was. 'Sorry, I didn't know.'

'It's the Caribbean, there's no need to be formal.' Would he be pushing his luck if he suggested that she remove the tight band holding her hair back, to pull her shirt out from her skirt? Probably.

Definitely.

'As I said, find me when you are done. I'll be around.' He felt his phone vibrate and then heard the personalised chirp telling him his assistant was looking for him. He walked away from Calla, hard to do, and pulled his phone from his pocket. That his PA was reaching out so soon after their last conversation meant that there was a crisis somewhere. *Crap.* Could he not have one day off?

Just one?

Calla wiggled her toes and sighed when she felt the blood flowing back into her cramped digits. She savoured the sun-warmed stone tiles beneath her feet, then walked over to the wall keeping her from falling the hundred feet down the cliff. Leaning on it, she rested her forearms and clasped her hands. She wanted to run, to catch a taxi back to the airport and return to Brooklyn, where she knew what she was doing. Well, sort of knew what she was doing. She hustled for work, tried to ignore her ex and did far more than she was asked for the clients she did manage to land, so that neither Jack nor Candice had any ammunition to use against her. So that she could always defend her work with complete conviction.

She turned around and lifted her eyes to take in the multilevel house. The tri-level Tuscan-style villa blended old world elegance with Caribbean appeal. Terracotta roof tiles, arched windows and weathered stucco walls gave the exterior a sun-warmed, Mediterranean vibe. This outdoor entertainment area, running the length of the house, was magnificent. It had three seating areas, couches in nineties flower prints close to the entrance, chairs under huge umbrellas next to the Jacuzzi and six loungers, two of which were double size, dotted around the pool. A sixteen-seater dining table occupied the space next to the Mexican-inspired outdoor kitchen, and next to it was a modern-looking bar with mirrors behind the fully stocked shelves.

It was a mishmash of styles and Calla wanted to get her hands on it. Desperately.

It was a crime to turn her back to the ocean, but she had to keep her eyes on the prize as she tried to make sense of her morning. She placed her hand on her too-fast heart and knew it was racing from a combination of excitement and confusion. Judah, the man who shattered her emotional equilibrium so easily ten months ago.

The same but so different: calm, commanding, flexing his confidence and wearing his power like a second skin. The contrast between the man he was then and now made her feel off balance and, yeah, rattled. Back then, with him, she'd felt weightless, like she was stepping into light and laughter. She'd found it so easy to talk to him, to let go, to *be*.

But the stakes were higher now, and she wasn't someone desperate to step out of her life. She wasn't as lost, as vulnerable. Scrabbling to reestablish her business, hustling for clients, working long hours had hardened and focused her, and she wasn't easily distracted. Yet he just needed to look at her from those lapis lazuli eyes and the ground shifted, rocking and rolling, beneath her.

It annoyed her that he still had an effect on her. Sure, he was a very good-looking, ripped, tall guy, but there had to be more to her reaction than a woman's appreciation for a hot man. She wasn't a teenager, for God's sake! So why did he still get under her skin? And why, dammit, did she desperately want to crawl into his arms, rest her head on his chest and *connect*?

She couldn't; that was impossible. And mixing sex and work would be a stupid thing to do. He was right—revamping Sol House would catapult her back into the big leagues. While she wasn't tempted (much) by the idea of becoming Reyes Luxe's in-house designer, a high-profile, international contract with Judah had the power to reset her entire reputation—under her own name, and on her own terms.

Stomping back to her tote bag, she pulled out her tablet and, still standing, jabbed the power button. After it booted up, she pulled up her old submission she sent to Judah's father last year. She scrolled through the images and renderings, wincing a little. They weren't bad; they had potential, but they were so damn *safe*. They lacked confidence and were tentative, a reflection of who she'd been at the time. With the distance of time, she knew they weren't good enough, and she wouldn't have, even if David Reyes hadn't collapsed, been awarded the contract. But she wasn't that designer anymore. She'd honed her skills, sharpened her pencils—metaphorically and literally—and was up to the challenge of Sol House. She could now handle anything life threw at her.

Including Judah Reyes. She'd be stepping into his world again, but this time she'd have boundaries. She'd keep their relationship purely professional, and her heart locked down and unaffected, her libido in check. She had to stay detached. And controlled. She couldn't afford to make the same mistake twice—not after Jack. Not after the humiliation of mixing business and love and having it blow up in her face. She'd lived that once. She would not allow that to happen to her again. And definitely not with Judah.

She was here to work. To prove to herself—and to everyone watching—that she could regain what Jack ripped from her and rebuild everything he tried to destroy. That she was still worthy. Still in control.

She was definitely not here to fail. Or to fall.

Well, there was no time like the present and no point in putting this off. Calla slid her tablet back into her tote bag and looked down at her discarded shoes. She loved the smooth stone of the floor under her feet. Judah's '*no shoes in the house*' decree meant she'd have to explore barefoot, forcing her to feel the house. She was very okay with that.

And, God, what a house.

Inside the great room, it was cool and quiet, reminding her of a grand old lady taking a nap. Even asleep, she oozed personality—hints of faded glamour, stubborn beauty and unapologetic originality.

Calla trailed her fingers along the edge of the

antique sideboard and took in the grand chandelier hanging from the ceiling. It was far too large and a little absurd in this Caribbean light, but somehow, it worked. Maybe it was the contradiction that made it interesting. Much like the man who now owned it.

This first walkthrough, without notes or a camera, was, despite everything that had happened, her favourite part of the process and the one thing Jack never managed to touch or taint. She cocked her head and listened to the house breathe, allowing it to be. To speak to her, if it wanted to. At the bottom of the staircase, a side table showed a long-forgotten deep white water ring. She could see the vase that once stood there: overflowing with lilies, lilacs, maybe garden roses. She could smell the floral scent trailing up the stairs behind someone barefoot and laughing, their tanned skin bearing hints of sea salt and sun. Someone happy. Someone *home*.

Despite everything, there was still joy in connecting with a property. She adored the house's soaring ceilings, the wrought iron details and the eclectic collection of art, from both Titans in the art world and those she thought might be island based. The upper-level guest suites were elegant but in need of attention. The gym boasted sleek top-of-the-line equipment. The wall panelling, however, needed to be ripped out and burned. It was dark, masculine and suffocating. Working out was hard enough; you didn't need to look at ugly walls while you punished yourself.

The kitchen—well, the less said about that, the better. And, ugh. It was all black stone and stainless steel—it felt like a catering kitchen. She opened one of the two eye-level ovens and frowned at its pristine condition. It didn't look like it had ever been used. She wrinkled her nose and climbed the staircase to the master suite.

Judah's scent hit her the second she stepped into his space.

It was still so familiar, an indefinable combination of spice, citrus…cedar? It was masculine, expensive and, infuriatingly, still the same smell she remembered from all those months ago. Trying to ignore the memories threatening to suck her in—of her putting her nose to his neck and inhaling him—she took in his bedroom, empty but for the absurdly large bed facing a wall of glass doors leading out onto a wraparound deck. From his bed, he could watch the ocean in all its moods.

Calla peeked into his walk-in closet and blinked. The man had more clothes than she did. Far too many shelves were dedicated to board shorts and even more to T-shirts in what she could only describe as designer monotony: navy, black, white, charcoal…

Shaking her head, a little amused, Calla walked out onto his private deck through the open glass doors next to the right side of his bed. Below her was a tropical garden bordering an immaculately maintained swathe of green grass. Walking around the corner, she put her back to that huge bed, and tried not to remember another bed in another place, a lot less opulent than this, but as sexy.

Don't go there, Calla. Sunlight dazzled off the sea, and the ocean breeze playfully tugged at her blouse. She rounded the corner and caught a glimpse of the stone terrace below, halfway down the cliff to the beach. On it, Judah's tall, broad frame moved with easy purpose. He was shirtless as he waxed a surfboard lying on a concrete table with wooden benches.

Her breath caught before she could stop it, her body remembering how he touched her, something her brain was desperate to forget. She narrowed her eyes, squinting against the glare. He looked relaxed, content. Not like a man who controlled a global company worth more millions than she could imagine.

He looked out to sea, and Calla followed his gaze, seeing the waves breaking offshore. Not the biggest, but surfable. If she didn't interrupt him now, she'd be stuck here until he came back. Which, judging from the memory of the last time, was long enough for her to wonder if he'd been swept out to sea.

If she was going to bid for this project, she had work to do and couldn't wait hours for him to come back. Her sketchbooks were still in her suite at the hotel. Her laptop, her pens—everything she needed was back there. But, before she could start, she needed to formally accept Judah's offer to submit her ideas.

Calla took a breath. Then another. Then marched barefoot back through Sol House and down to the terrace, hoping she could keep her spine straight and her heart in check.

Calla's pulse pounded as she wandered down the path that would eventually lead to the private beach cove. She stopped at the edge of the stone terrace halfway down, her eyes on Judah standing next to a long, well-used surfboard, applying wax with slow, practised strokes.

The breath snagged in her throat. She knew what she was doing with paint samples, and fabrics, with textures and perspective, but she had no idea how to handle this muscular man with shadows in his eyes. His skin glowed warm and golden, the ridges of his back flexing with each movement. He didn't look like a CEO. Nor did he look like the man who'd handed her a massive opportunity in an '*Iced Americano to go*' voice.

Right now, he looked like he did that night. Like the man who'd walked her out of the hotel and kissed her like he already knew how she'd taste.

He looked up, eyes shaded by the sun, but that crooked half-smile she remembered, the one she found so sexy, lifted the corners of his mouth.

'You were a while,' he commented.

'Mm. There was a lot of house to explore.' She folded her arms, ignoring the way her fingers itched to brush the swoosh of sand off his left shoulder. His damp board shorts suggested he'd already taken a dip. She was jealous; the sea looked cool and inviting. But then she remembered it was June, the height of summer, and would probably be the temperature of barely heated soup. 'I didn't expect to find you out here.'

Judah wiped his hands on a towel and stood, tall and barefoot, lifted the board off the bench and planted its tip in the sand next to his foot. 'I took a call, sent a few emails and decided that it was too beautiful a day to be inside.'

'How often do you get to come out to the island?' she asked, running her toe up and down the back of her bare calf. She felt a little silly standing barefoot, her shirt still carefully tucked into the band of her tight-fitting skirt, with strands of her hair escaping from her sleek tail. She tucked them behind her ears.

He glanced out at the horizon to where the water shimmered like a sheet of polished blue glass. ‘I haven’t been back since that weekend.’

She waggled a finger between his chest and hers. ‘Since we…’

‘Yeah.’ He sighed and rubbed his shoulder blade, the one free of sea sand. ‘I flew in a couple of days ago.’ Yet instead of taking the time to settle in, he’d invited her out to get working on his house. Why so soon? Why hadn’t he taken a few days to decompress?

‘I’m still getting into the rhythm of being here, the pace of the island,’ Judah added.

She lifted her hand. ‘The island has a pace?’ she asked. ‘What is it called? One beat faster than sleepy?’

He smiled, and Calla’s stomach flipped over. God, the combination of his quirking lips, flash of white teeth and the shallow dimple in his stubble could liquefy knees at fifty paces.

‘I’ve decided to take your job offer,’ she said, hearing the tremble in her voice and hating it.

‘I’m sure that you’d prefer your client to be anyone but me.’

She bit the inside of her lip and forced herself to meet his enigmatic eyes. ‘A client is a client,’ she murmured.

‘Liar,’ Judah softly retorted. ‘You hate the personal connection.’

She couldn't deny it, and a part of her wanted to insist that nothing personal remained between them—that she'd feel the same way if he were any other man. She didn't have time for complications, romantic or personal, because she had to focus on growing her company and proving Jack and the Abernathy clan wrong. That she was talented, reliable and responsible. That she belonged in the world they ruled. And the only way she could do that was by landing a big whale client. They didn't get much bigger than Judah Reyes.

'So you're willing to give it a shot?'

'Yes, despite the surprise reunion. Despite the...' She sighed, looking for the right words. 'Despite everything.' The memories, the potential emotional landmines she'd have to dodge. She couldn't pass this up; she'd regret it forever if she did.

Something flickered in Judah's gaze. Relief?

'Good.' He handed her a sharp nod. 'Professionally, I'll give you all the input you need. I want you to bring the house back to life.'

By qualifying his statement, by sliding in the word *professionally*, he made her think of that iceberg again, of strong currents underneath a calm surface. What was she missing? The best way to find out was to ask. She narrowed her eyes. 'And personally?'

He stepped closer, careful, and she wondered where he'd go next, whether he'd tell her the truth or brush over her question. He was now so close she could feel heat rolling off him, see the faint scar on his collarbone, the exact line where the stubble on his neck stopped, his individual, surprisingly long eyelashes. But up close, she could also see his exhaustion, and the muted emotion in his eyes a direct contrast to the amusement and mischief she remembered.

'Personally,' he said, voice lower now, 'I remember every moment we spent together—I remember how you were. Open. Unfiltered. Real. I'm wondering if that woman I met is simply buried behind your straight hair and businesslike clothes, or whether she's gone forever.'

He didn't need to know that when she returned from St Croix, she, very deliberately, very systematically, took her beach clothes, the bikini she wore, her flip-flops and every memory of Judah, and the person she'd been with him, and packed them away. She'd had a life to rebuild, pride to salvage, and she hadn't wanted to be distracted by recollecting a never-to-be-seen again blue-eyed surfer who'd rocked her world.

Guess she was super wrong about that.

Her heart kicked against her ribs. 'A lot has happened since we last connected, Judah. And that weekend was a way for me to step out of my life. I didn't have anything to lose back then.'

And if they got personal, if they decided to re-explore their attraction—and when he looked at her like that, she knew he was as attracted to her as she was to him—she would carry the majority of the risk. If it ended badly—and these types of situations always ended badly—Judah could, very easily, find another designer, but she'd fail to restore her reputation and she'd lose future work. She was the one carrying all the risk.

'Can we forget what we did, who we were?' she asked, stepping back and hauling in a deep breath. 'I can't go back, Judah. I *won't* go back.'

He exhaled and pushed a frustrated hand through his hair, his lips thinning. 'Sorry, *shit*.' He grimaced. 'I told myself I wasn't going to bring it up—I was going to leave well alone—but seeing you all buttoned up annoys me. I'm trying to be more of this—' he gestured to himself, bare-chested, board at his feet, wind tugging at his hair '—and less of the Reyes Luxe version.'

He'd lost her. 'I don't understand.'

He managed a small smile. 'I don't blame you. I barely understand it myself.' He took a moment, obviously trying to make sense of his thoughts. 'This island is my favourite place, the place where I can *be*. As my designer, I'd like you to embrace the island and the house. And I don't want you designing for the brand. I want you to design for *me*.'

The words landed hard, too close to vulnerability. They were too intimate.

'I also want you to stay on the property.'

He wanted her to live and work in his house? She stared at him, and a warning light whirled in her brain, red and flashing. No, she needed the distance and safety of being able to leave each day, to return to her hotel room to recalibrate. How could she work, concentrate, when she had to spend so much time with her sexy client and the ex-lover she'd tried so very hard to forget?

Calla looked away, toward the water. 'That's not a good idea, Judah. You *know* it's not.'

Stubbornness jumped into his eyes. 'I'd like you to live on-site. I asked Bella to make up the guest cottage for you.'

The guest cottage was one step removed from staying in his house, but still…

'Judah—'

'That's the deal, Calla.'

'You keep changing the goal posts,' she cried. 'You're making me jump through hoops because you know how much I want and need this project.'

He didn't back down and, once again, despite his bare chest and sand- and sun-dusted shoulders, she saw the determined man who operated an international empire. 'You can either stay in a guest suite in the house, or in the guest cottage. Your choice.'

Calla knew there was no point in arguing; he wasn't going to back down. And this wasn't a hill she was prepared to die on. She silently cursed him before pushing her words out between gritted teeth. 'I'll move into the guest cottage.'

But she needed to remind him of her boundaries and where they were. 'We need to keep this clean, Judah.' A memory flashed in his eyes. She knew it—something that reminded him of the wonderfully dirty-in-the-best-way-possible sex they'd shared. She needed to clarify her statement. Immediately. 'We need to be professional.'

He tipped his head in a gesture that might, if she tried hard to see it that way, be one of agreement. Calla's breath caught at the heat in his eyes. She was very out of practice, but she recognised desire and lust when it burned super brightly. And all for her. And damn her for wanting to slide over to him, to hoist her thigh over his hip, to place her hands on his shoulders and kiss him stupid.

Stop. Enough now.

Calla turned away. She needed distance. Space. Boundaries. She glanced at the guest cottage, set a little way apart from the main house. It wasn't enough, but it would have to do.

She started to climb the stone path back up to the house, away from him and her attraction, but couldn't stop herself from glancing back at him, once.

And of course, he was watching her, his gaze heating her skin as it always did.

'Calla.'

She turned. Judah leaned the surfboard against the table and put his hands on his hips. It was a classic warrior pose and was accompanied by a frown and a hard jaw. 'As I said, it's strictly business for as long as you want it to be.'

He covered this distance between them in a couple of strides, stepped into her personal space and ducked his head. When he spoke again, his breath tickled the hair at her temple and drifted over her ear. 'But do let me know if you want that to change.'

Calla cursed the heat in her cheeks and wished she could be half as direct, as confident as he was. She might be older in years, but he had her beat when it came to self-possession. 'I don't know what to say to that,' she admitted.

Judah smiled, walked away from her, and Calla watched him go, her bottom lip caught between her teeth. What the hell had just happened? And why did her heart feel like it was beating at a thousand beats per second? Why did crazy things always seem to happen to her?

But most of all, why did she feel like running into Judah Reyes here in St Croix was utterly, illogically *right*? Like meeting him again was going to change her life in ways big and small?

CHAPTER THREE

STANDING TO ONE side of Judah's entertainment deck, a little apart from the rest of his guests, Calla sipped her mojito and sent a wistful look toward the guest house. She'd been at Sol House for two days, sleeping in the cottage for one, and she didn't want to spend the evening socialising with people she didn't know. What she most wanted to do was to change into a bikini and amble down to the beach for a night swim. Or to lie in her bed next to the open window, under the fan, listening to the waves roll up onto the rocks below the cliff as she studied the summer night sky.

This party was, so Judah informed her when he arrived at the cottage yesterday to issue the invitation, an island tradition, one his mom started over thirty years ago and which had grown into an annual affair. Judah'd said he could still picture them, his mother radiant as she greeted guests, his captivated father never far from her side. Calla imagined that Sol House, and his childhood, had pulsed with joy on those warm St Croix nights, the air tinged with sea brine, champagne and expensive scents.

Judah's guests were a mixture of islanders, expats and business friends. Some guests had flown in just to attend his summer party—a clear reminder of how influential he was. There had to be over a hundred people in attendance, scattered through the house and gardens, drinking his champagne and keeping his hired-for-the-night bartenders and caterers busy.

There were some big names here—some Calla hadn't expected to see—and it reminded her that while Judah was based in London, he was as influential in New York. She watched an important art curator glide past, her hand tucked into the arm of a Manhattan power player rumoured to dabble in black market art. A few former clients had recognised Calla—people she and Jack had once worked with—and their curiosity was obvious. She and Jack had each been a half of Atelier Abernathy—they'd started the business together, but in their divorce, Jack treated it like it was all his—but in a world that made sense, Jack should be here, not her.

Throughout the evening, she'd sensed eyes on her, saw how people abruptly stopped talking when she looked their way. She'd somehow become the talk of the party, a huge curiosity.

Calla sighed. People loved unanswered questions, and when it was accompanied by a hint of scandal—the dissolution of their marriage and the interior design studio they owned together had been gossip gold and kept tongues wagging for the best part of a year—all the better.

Her phone buzzed in her hand, a sharp interruption to the low hum of music and laughter floating over the pool.

She glanced at the screen. There was one new message.

Are you enjoying Reyes's party? Have you found someone to talk to? Probably not—because we both know you don't belong there. You belong here, working behind the scenes, under me. *For me.*

Calla exhaled slowly through her nose. Jack. Naturally. Having lived with her for so long, he knew exactly how to weaponise her insecurity. He'd always had an uncanny talent for finding the softest, rawest part of her and twisting the knife. She locked the screen without replying, shoving her phone back into the pocket of her wrap dress.

What was it with Jack and his inability to let go? Why couldn't he just…unhook himself from her life and fade away? Why was he still obsessed with her, with what she was doing? More importantly, why hadn't she blocked him? Why did she keep hanging on to him, even if it was by the messages he sent?

She'd told herself it was strategic—that through his messages, Jack frequently dropped hints about what was happening in the design world she ached to be a part of and cutting him off meant cutting herself off from that world. But maybe, deep down, she wanted to believe that one day the man she'd married, loved, would turn out to be better, kinder. Nicer. Maybe she was looking for a reason to justify giving him a decade of her life.

Calla slipped into the shadows, partially concealed by a column and a huge ficus tree, happy to separate herself from the too-brittle laughter and the rising noise. Through the leaves, she scanned the crowds of threes and fours, looking for Judah. Because he was so tall, she found him quickly. She liked his outfit. The lightweight, milk chocolate–coloured trousers, sockless brogues and a cream linen shirt, sleeves rolled up his forearms, suited him.

Sometimes when he tipped his head to the side, when he half smiled, she saw the younger man she spent the night with, the carefree surfer who made her laugh, sigh and scream. But he was definitely more distant than before, cautious and careful. The past months had changed him: he'd aged. Oh, not physically, but mentally, emotionally. He'd taken an emotional battering. Having been through one herself, she could recognise the signs from miles away.

Back then, he seemed much younger than her, the six-year gap between them so much wider than it was today. Now it seemed inconsequential. If anything, she felt like he was older, definitely harder, tougher. Not prepared to take any shit. And damn, that made him more attractive, not less.

'I've wanted to kiss you since the second I saw you. I kept thinking, no way it'll be as good as I imagine...'

He leaned in, and moonlight emphasised the light stubble on his strong jaw. 'You're like sailing through the Drake Passage during an Antarctic storm, thrilling and dangerous. Kiss me again.'

Nothing could stop her, and she did.

Her hands slid up his chest, fingers splaying over warm solid muscle, and her body moved instinctively into his. And oh, God, this man could kiss.

Judah kissed like a man who knew he was good at it. He took his time, kissed her deep, then light, then deep again, alternating between devastating hunger and exquisite tenderness. It was maddening. It was glorious. He built her up until her skin vibrated with tension...and then he pulled back, just enough to keep her right on the edge. Frustrating, yes—but soul-tinglingly, deliciously right.

This was what she hadn't even realised she was missing. Not just from her marriage but from the few men she dated before Jack. None of them had made her feel like this.

Like her skin was too tight for her body, and her heart was warm honey. Everything in the world contracted to where their bodies met—their mouths, hands, his warm, masculine body, his hard erection, pressing against her stomach. Judah made her feel intensely, astonishingly feminine. *More herself than she'd ever been. Younger, hotter, cooler, he made her feel everything she should as a woman.*

And everything she shouldn't.

Annoyed with herself for falling into the memory, Calla turned her back to him and rested her arms on the veranda railing, her eyes on the sea far below her. The colour of the night sky was an inky, deep vibrant blue, the same shade as Judah's eyes. It was a colour she wanted to use as an accent shade. In the library, maybe? Or the master bathroom?

'Why is she here and not Jack Abernathy?'

Calla stiffened as the coated-with-spite words

drifted over to her. The speaker was standing off to the side and hadn't noticed her. In her black dress, she blended into the shadows.

'I can't understand why Judah would employ a talentless nobody whose only claim to fame is marrying Jack. Everybody knows that Jack carried her, that he's the design genius behind Atelier Abernathy. His design for the Metfords' mansion was a work of art.'

Calla slapped her hand over her mouth to keep her snort from escaping. Yeah, Jack's contribution to that job had been to flirt with Mrs Metford and to explain Calla's ideas. She'd been the one who'd burned the midnight oil, who'd tracked down the unusual architectural elements, commissioned the once-off furniture and designed the fabrics. But Jack, because he was a master manipulator and the King of Spin, took all the credit for her hard work.

'His pro bono upgrade of the kids' paediatric ward at Cummings Hospital was also genius. It was part fantasy, part practical, all fun.' Okay, that comment hurt more. That project had been a heart tugger, something she poured everything she had into.

Calla heard a distinctively feminine sniff. 'And what did she do? Messed up on contracts, cheated on him and rode his coattails. God, how did he hook up with such a talentless hack?'

Calla dropped to her haunches and placed her head in the crook of her arms. She'd been talked about incessantly ever since the divorce and company break-up, and she knew people had said worse about her than this. But, God, why did it still hurt so much?

Jack had stolen her work, sabotaged her reputation and painted her as unstable, and she was still suffering from his emotional brutality. Was it any wonder that she'd vowed never to trust again, that she'd never risk losing everything again? Love was the most destructive weapon out there.

More importantly, what should she do now? Stand up and make her presence known? Keep her position and hide?

'Ladies.'

Calla lifted her head at Judah's pointed drawl. She stiffened. Did he know she was here? Still on her haunches, she shuffled backwards, closer to the railing, deeper into the shadows. She could just see his bare ankle, his big foot, the cuff of his fashionably short pants.

'What a lovely party, gorgeous champagne. We're having a lovely time.'

Yeah, that voice was pitched lower than before and carried a great deal of flirt. Judah took a moment to respond. 'That's strange—I didn't think you were enjoying yourselves.'

Calla's eyebrows lifted at his comment. Judging by the feminine gasps, they were equally surprised by his observation. 'Really? Why on earth would you think that?' one of them asked.

'People having fun don't stand in dark corners gossiping about their fellow guests.'

The silence following his statement was thick with embarrassment. 'Ah…*um*.'

Judah's tone dropped a couple of degrees. 'You're an art curator, right? And you're a gallery owner?' he said, his tone silky. Calla shivered. Why did she feel like she preferred to be hiding in the shadows rather than standing in front of him?

'Yes, we are,' Viper One replied, introducing herself and her companion. 'It's so nice to meet you, Judah.'

'Did I invite you?'

'Um, we tagged along with the Streatfields—they own a villa on the North Shore. We were just talking about your art, and were wondering if you'd—'

'You were not talking art—you were trashing one of my guests, who happens to be my super-talented interior designer, Calla West.'

Calla's eyes widened. Instead of apologising or even acknowledging Judah's accusation, the blonde took her shot to make her pitch. 'I'd love to talk to you about loaning some of the art you inherited from your father to my gallery—'

Viper Two wasn't about to be outdone and outmanoeuvred. 'And if you are looking for something special, I am deeply connected to the art world.'

Wow, they weren't shy.

Judah stepped back, and Calla leaned forward, just a little, to see him. She took in his hard, you're-dead-to-me death stare. He jerked his head toward the exit. 'You have five minutes to leave. If you don't, I will get my people to escort you out. I will make it obvious you are no longer welcome here.'

Under their perma-tans, they paled. They looked at each other, confused. 'But why?'

'Nobody insults *my* people in *my* house at *my* party. Leave. *Now.*'

They scuttled away like beach crabs caught beneath the light of a handheld torch. Calla watched as Judah closed his eyes, gripped the bridge of his nose and sighed. 'Will this damned party ever end?' he muttered.

Her thoughts exactly. Calla watched as he rolled his shoulders and tipped his head from side to side, as if trying to gather some energy to keep going. Then he swivelled around and walked over to her, holding out his hand. Judging by his lack of hesitation, he'd known she was there the whole time.

When she placed hers in his, so much bigger, he tugged her to her feet. 'Are you okay?' he demanded, his tone low. Calla was grateful his big body shielded her from the guests behind him.

She pushed her hair behind her ears. 'I'm fine,' she replied, embarrassed.

He narrowed his eyes, disbelief crossing his face. 'You are not,' he disagreed. Liking her hand in his a little too much, Calla pulled it away and folded her arms across her chest. Whether she was fine or not didn't matter; she was here to do a job and she couldn't let him see how rattled she was.

'Want to tell me what that was all about?' Judah demanded.

She'd rather have her fingers smashed. 'It's nothing.'

'Don't treat me like an idiot, Calla.'

There was a hard, don't-mess-with-me note in his voice she'd never heard before. Something lethal and unforgiving. 'I don't like being lied to,' he stated.

She didn't either. She wrinkled her nose. 'I have what some would term an ugly relationship with my ex-business partner and husband,' she explained. 'He has his supporters.' Which would include pretty much anyone with any clout in Manhattan.

'Mr Slick from the bar?'

His gaze sliced through her—cool, steady, unblinking. His expression remained implacable, but his eyes told a different story: the holes in her explanation were wide enough to sail a container ship through sideways.

'Thank you for standing up for me,' she said. It had been so long since someone had taken her side, and she felt tears burning her eyes and the back of her throat. 'I appreciate it.' His defence of her had been quiet but lethal, and he'd handled the ugly situation with sharp efficiency and subtlety.

'I don't need to be thanked,' he brusquely replied, jamming his hands into the pockets of his pants. 'And don't you dare cry—you're too strong and have too much pride to let those hyenas affect you.'

His words were bullet harsh, but she lifted her chin to meet his eyes. He held her gaze for a few beats, then nodded. 'Yes, there's your spine. Good job, Calla.'

Calla pulled in some air, unable to break his intense stare. She was so drawn to his steadiness and liked that he could see both her vulnerability and her strength. But then fear rolled over her, a cold North Atlantic storm surge. She'd allowed a man to see those sides of her before, allowed him into her heart and mind, gave him her body, and he'd stomped all over her in his Guiseppe Zanotti shoes. She'd never allow a man that much power over her again.

Judah sighed. 'And she's gone.' He rubbed the back of his neck. 'I liked the woman I met last year. Can I have her back again?'

'That was one night and a day, never to be repeated,' Calla told him.

'Pity,' Judah drawled. 'I liked her. A lot.'

She'd liked that person too. But that night had been a step out of time; it hadn't been real life. They'd shoved the world away and had played, laughed and loved in an alternate reality. Those golden hours could never be sustained long-term. Open, eager, chatty, quick to laugh, she'd let her guard down, piece by piece, and lived like there had been no tomorrow. But when she woke up from an afternoon nap, sunlight streaming in from the window and the cries of the gulls fighting over a crab, she knew that it was over. Real life needed to be faced so as she dressed, she picked up the bricks and the barbed wire and re-created all her emotional barriers. With one last look at Judah, naked, lying on his stomach, all golden skin and ripped muscles, she'd walked away, knowing he'd only ever be a brief, amazing experience, an incredible memory.

But here he was, having hauled her back into his life, back to this place. And this time she couldn't leave. This time, for the sake of her company, her pride and her reputation, she had to stick. And stay.

'I'd love to know what you are thinking,' Judah murmured.

Before she could answer, someone called his name. He lifted his hand in acknowledgement and sighed. 'Go to bed—get some sleep. It's been a long day,' he told her, his tone suggesting she not argue. Man, he'd perfected his ordering-his-underlings, CEO-in-charge voice. But Calla found herself nodding. There was nothing she wanted more.

Well, maybe to have him in her bed with her... no! *Jeez, Calla, get a grip.*

Immediately!

CHAPTER FOUR

THE NEXT EVENING, Calla sat in the corner of a couch in Judah's great room and watched her first tropical storm batter the cliffs and the cove below them. Just an hour ago, Judah tracked her down and insisted she come up to the main house, telling her that a tropical storm had abruptly changed course and its outer edges would slap this side of the island and Sol House. It wasn't safe for her to be alone if the storm intensified. She'd tried to protest, but Judah remained firm; he wanted her in the big house.

She'd thought he was overreacting, but the sea, which glittered playfully that morning, turned a sullen grey-green, spitting restless waves onto the rocks and Judah's private beach. The air slowly grew heavier, thickened with humidity and electric tension. Clouds gathered, a slow-moving army—thick, low and slate-coloured—dragging gloom across the sky. The gusty wind tossed branches, rattled shutters and bent trees. It wasn't a storm at its strongest, ugliest or angriest, but it was enough to set her nerves on edge. She winced as lightning slashed the sky wide open, white-hot and furious. A beat later, thunder boomed, and she slapped her hands over her ears, her heart punching her ribs.

Judah nudged her shoulder with the foot of a wine glass. 'The storm is still offshore,' he said. 'But even being on the edges of it can feel like standing between chaos coming in and chaos going out.

'Here, it's decent red—it'll calm your nerves.' Calla took the glass, her fingers grazing his—warm, callused, familiar—and turned her gaze to the roiling sky.

Chaos in and chaos out. That was a good description of their relationship. They were suspended in the in-between. Memory and want behind them, questions and confusion ahead. Too much history to go back. Too little certainty to move forward. And no map for what came next.

Judah sat down on the opposite edge of the couch and propped his bare feet up onto the glass, steel and wood coffee table in front of him. They'd lost power a half hour ago, and then the generator immediately kicked in. But Judah killed all the lights, telling her that the best way to watch a storm was with the house in darkness. She didn't tell him that the last thing she wanted to do was sit in the dark and watch nature throw a temper tantrum.

Good things never happened on stormy nights.

'You're more tense than I expected you to be,' Judah said, looking relaxed. But his sharp eyes were on her face, and Calla knew he was looking for an explanation as to why her shoulders were up around her ears and her hand was tightly clenched around the stem of her wine glass.

She couldn't tell him that she'd once loved storms, that she'd been the girl who'd run out into the rain to dance, the thunder the only music she needed. She'd whirl and twirl and kick puddles of water, arms akimbo, a huge smile on her face. But then, a few weeks after she turned nineteen, her dad died during a storm and, many years later, Jack, his voice raised above the sound of hail and thunder, told her he was divorcing her, that there was no money left in their joint personal and business accounts, her beloved company was a hollowed-out empty shell and her reputation was in tatters. She'd wanted to howl, but the wind outside did it for her, a wild animal caught in a situation with no escape. Each lightning strike was a knife in her heart, each roll of thunder spiking her soul. Jack just sat there, a smirk on his face, enjoying the havoc and destruction.

She recalled wondering why she never knew

how much he hated her, how much he resented her. She hadn't seen it...no, she'd *chosen* not to see it. He'd snowed her, but she'd let him.

She was no longer the girl who loved storms; she would never dance in the rain again. Calla lifted her wine glass to her lips and took a long swallow, then another. A lightning strike, closer this time, made her glass wobble, and the red wine sloshed in her glass. Judah's fingers covered hers, and he slid the glass from her grip and placed it on the table in front of her. He scooted closer to her and half turned to face her. 'The storm is about five miles from here. We're only experiencing the outer edges. The lightning is a long way away, the thunder too. When dawn breaks, it's going to be another stunning summer's day in the Caribbean, utterly calm.'

Yeah, but it was a long time between now and then. And anything could happen.

'It's also moving away from us.'

'It doesn't feel like it,' she muttered. Sheet lightning threw light onto the shadows in the room, and the sea roared below them. Thunder rattled the glass in the windows, and the wind skittered over the house, making the shutters shudder.

'Tell me what you remember about that night we spent together,' Judah said, placing a hand on the foot she'd tucked under her thigh. She sent a fearful glance out the window. Calla thought about pulling her foot out from under his hand, but his touch settled her, made her feel safe. And grounded. Like nothing could happen to her while Judah held her, his fingers wrapped around her slender foot, his thumb sliding over the skin on the arch of her foot. But as his words settled, she squirmed.

There was so much else they could talk about, so why was he going there, going back?

Why couldn't they ignore it and pretend it never happened? And why was it that the one night she let her guard down—really let it down, his-kisses-on-her-skin, laughed-so-hard-she-cried, was-thoroughly-loved kind of down—was with him?

Judah *bloody* Reyes.

And just like before, he still affected her. His mouth. The way he walked, looked and smiled. The way his voice wrapped around her like a heated blanket and made her think stupid things, like *maybe you're safe here*. She wasn't safe anywhere, nor with anyone.

That old version of her? The one tangled in those sheets, whispering to a stranger with cobalt blue eyes? She didn't exist outside of that one night. Calla couldn't afford to. Too much was riding on her being professional, emotionally distant and in control.

This person she was now wore heels, severe suits and three layers of emotional protection. She read every email, contract and memo twice, and didn't believe in fate or chemistry or whatever nonsense that made women fall into bed with men like him. But Judah was back in her life looking at her like he knew something. Like he'd seen her without the mask and remembered the woman underneath. He'd seen her in ways no one else ever had. Him looking at her like *that*, and the way she reacted, was dangerous. She couldn't go back to that night, and wouldn't allow herself to go to him again. Not when everything she'd built was hanging on her staying in control. She cleared her throat and told herself—again—that she had to focus on the job. His high-profile, make-or-break, life-changing opportunity. Offered to her by the only man who ever made her forget her name.

Why was life messing with her?

'I don't see the point of looking back, Judah,' she said, pulling her foot out from under his hand and placing her feet on the floor, her knees pressed together.

'You're like a prickly hedgehog who curls up into a spiky ball when it's threatened.'

It wasn't a bad analogy. Not that she'd tell him that. 'I just think we should keep our relationship confined to business,' she stated, wincing at her too-prim voice. God, was this how she sounded all the time? Uptight and prissy and unapproachable?

'That's difficult to do since I clearly remember what you look like naked, the sounds you made as I loved you, the way you called my name when you fell apart.'

Calla lifted her hand to her forehead, heat starting as a small flicker and exploding into a supernova. Why did he have to remind her of how good they'd been together? Memories rushed over her, recollections of him holding the side of her face with his big hand, his eyes locked on hers as he pushed into her, the perfection of that moment, the suggestion that she'd been created to be loved by him, just like that.

Her eyes crashed into his, and electricity, borrowed from the lightning, arced between them, as powerful as anything nature could generate. It took all her willpower not to lean against his broad chest, his arms around her, to rest a minute within the safety of his grasp. But she wouldn't allow herself to be that weak, to fall apart.

She couldn't trust him to hold her. Not for long anyway.

Calla pushed to her feet and slid her feet into her sandals. She pressed her fingers to her thumb—index, middle, ring, pinkie—and the repeated motion soothed her, bringing her back to the moment and what was important. The storm, both inside her and on the other side of the massive windows, was dying down, and her moment of weakness, of temptation—an old-fashioned word but apt—had passed.

She was back in control. And control was everything.

As if to put an exclamation mark at the end of that thought, the hum of the generator disappeared, telling her the power had been restored. Calla raked her hair back and pasted a small smile on her face. 'I'm going to head back to the cottage and get some work done,' she told him, ignoring his penetrating gaze.

'Is this who you are now?' he softly asked.

'What do you mean?'

'Do you simply ignore the uncomfortable because it's exactly that...uncomfortable?'

Well, yes. Because she didn't know how to answer, Calla just shrugged. 'Doesn't everyone?'

'Sit down, Calla, and finish your wine.'

Judah leaned back, trying not to make it too obvious that he was watching her, because the last thing he wanted was to spook her more than she already was. But damn, keeping his eyes off her felt like he was asking the tide not to turn. There was something magnetic about her, something in the way she held herself that made it impossible to look away. Like she'd packed her whole damn history into her petite, compact frame and dared the world to guess how heavy it was. He wouldn't pretend to know the weight of it. He just knew she carried it like it didn't cost her anything, which probably meant it cost her a lot more than she'd wanted to pay.

She resumed her perch on the edge of the couch, a skittish bird about to take flight. She was, but wasn't, the same woman from that night. This Calla was the edge of a sharpened blade, the fine tip of a fountain pen. The Great Wall of China in human form.

But she was still her. Or was he simply hoping, praying the woman he remembered still existed under all her many layers? Because if that held true, then there was a chance that the man he used to be, joyful and relaxed, quick to laugh, was also still buried—barely breathing but alive—under the layers of expectation and responsibility and the Reyes Luxe brand.

He reached for his wine glass. Sipped it slowly and said nothing for a while. The sound of the storm moving out to sea filled the silence.

She turned to look at him, her shoulders and back stiff. 'Why are you doing this, Judah? Why are you raking up the past?' she demanded, sounding a little desperate. 'Why did you even ask me here? What do you want from me?'

He rubbed his forehead with his fingertips. Wasn't that the question? It had been, still was, irrational and absurd, but he couldn't shake the idea that being near her again might help him claw his way back to that version of himself. Being back in St Croix—with Calla at his side—felt like he might finally stumble across the answers he'd been looking for.

'That's a difficult question to answer.'

Judah resisted the urge to run his thumb over those too-deep lines between her arched eyebrows.

Her deep eyes slammed into his. 'I need to know... How much is my being here, on the island, about the time we spent together? Is this about work or what happened back then?'

He'd been dreading this question and didn't know how to answer her. And he had to be careful; if he messed up now, their working relationship—any relationship—would be over before it started. He ran his thumb over his jaw, his stubble scratchy.

'I wouldn't have asked you to submit a proposal if I didn't think you were the right fit,' Judah said, his voice steady. 'This house...it means something to me, it's been in my family for decades. My mother used to fall asleep in that hammock in the garden during the summer heat. I learned to swim right off this beach. It's more than a building—it's part of me. I wouldn't hand it over to just anyone.' He paused, his eyes holding hers. 'I've seen your portfolio, and I looked into your past work. I liked what I saw—more than liked it. You've got talent, Calla. Real vision. And that's what Sol House deserves.'

'Then why won't you let me do my job without complicating it with references to the past? Why do you keep dragging it up?'

Because it was a compass point, something he held on to, a lighthouse when the swell rose and the winds whipped. Because it was the memory that comforted and consoled him, that anchored him.

Judah resisted the urge to scrub his hands over his face. They were still finding their way back to each other, not yet comfortable, and the months since he'd last seen her seemed like years. Calla crossed her arms, her fingertips digging into her biceps. She wasn't ready, or prepared, to broach their past, or to hear about his other reason for wanting her in St Croix. Then again, he wasn't ready to tell her.

Because he hadn't worked out how to say, 'That thirty-six hours with you? That was the last time I felt like myself.'

And maybe a part of him wanted her to see him as controlled, together, an adult. Back then, he'd let her believe he was just some barefoot bartender. A man with no ambition or direction. He'd treated her like he did everyone else, thinking it was safer to be underestimated than to create expectations that, as the son of David Reyes, he couldn't meet.

He was a Reyes. The only Reyes of Reyes Luxe. She now knew he was responsible for the company his father had built. But she didn't know that most days he was holding on by his fingernails, trying not to get chewed up by it. And if he explained, would she be disappointed? Worse, far worse, would she pity him? He couldn't handle that. He wanted her to see him as solid. Capable. Completely confident. Not the guy who sometimes still felt he was surfing a monster wave, waiting to be crushed.

'I need to get going,' she said. 'I still have work I want to do tonight.'

It was blatantly obvious she wasn't ready to remember, to go back. So he stood there, hands in his pockets to hide his clenched fists, and gave her what she obviously wanted, the polished and professional version of himself. Judah Reyes in all his CEO glory. 'Right, we're keeping things professional.'

Judah gave her a tight smile, knowing that it didn't reach his eyes. 'The storm has moved out to sea, and any danger has long passed,' he said. 'Do you want me to walk you back to the cottage?' He knew she'd refuse, but manners dictated that he ask.

'I'm fine.'

Of course, she was. 'I'll see you in the morning.'

He lifted his chin and pulled up his most implacable expression. By the time she murmured a soft goodnight, he'd slipped back into his corporate skin, back into being the version of Judah Reyes who didn't show his hand, who'd never let anyone see he was off balance. Someone determined to learn how to wrangle his empire, isolation and uncertainties alone.

Calla curled up on the overstuffed daybed in the guest house, her coffee cup resting on her thigh. The distant thunder and the occasional howl from the wind reminded her that the storm still swirled somewhere out to sea. But the storm in her soul was louder. Messier.

She exhaled, emotionally and physically whipped, and stared out into the smudgy darkness. Damn, Judah. What was all that about?

His question put her on a remote highway in the dark, about to be run over by an eighteen-wheeler truck. She hadn't the first idea how to react. Then, when she'd tried to pull them back to work and business, he shut down immediately, pulling back and away.

His expression haunted her. He hadn't tried to argue or explain, hadn't pushed for more. He'd simply...*stopped*. Shut down and retreated. She exhaled and stared out into the smudgy dark. And wasn't she being a hypocrite? On one hand, she wanted him to push her, on the other, she wanted him to be professional. That wasn't right. Or fair. But she vacillated between the two with all the enthusiasm of an out-of-control bungee rope.

Calla wrapped her hands around the coffee cup, trying to absorb its dwindling warmth. She hated the unreadable look in his eyes, his tight smile, the way he'd offered to walk her back as if they were strangers—the prick was sharper than she wanted to admit. He'd uttered that line about being professional, handing her what she asked for. Professionalism. Distance. Detachment. So why did it feel like a door had slammed inside her chest?

It was for the best. She needed to keep a healthy distance between them because there was too much at stake. Her career, her reputation, her need for control.

Calla stood up, walked to the tiny kitchenette, tossed her cold coffee into the sink and placed the cup in the dishwasher. She should've walked away from him, refused to listen and kept it professional.

'Judah, you and I…we were a moment, a step out of time. An anomaly,' she whispered, her chest tight. She hoped saying the words aloud would make them settle and lodge in her soul. 'A bright, burning blip.'

So then why did she feel she was standing in a hot, too-bright spotlight? She wanted to be furious and dug deep to find her anger. When she did track it down, it was muted and laced with regret, confusion and a gnawing question she couldn't shake: Was he really as emotionally composed as he wanted her to believe? And why, *really*, had he brought her to St Croix?

And why did a part of her want to remember the woman she so briefly was? The one who could laugh easily, talk openly and be emotionally available? Calla walked into the bedroom, feeling like a zinc bathtub riding the white water rapids of a too-fast river. Judah—an emotionally available alpha male, a rare and dangerous breed—wasn't someone she was ready, or able, to deal with.

'Next time, let's keep it professional.'

She tested the words, hoping to sound like she meant it. She didn't, the tremble in her voice too distinct. Going forward, could she do that?

She didn't know.

CHAPTER FIVE

A COUPLE OF days later, Judah placed his hands on the long dining table outside and stared down at her sketches, taking in her mood board and her colour combinations. Calla could read his body language and knew he wasn't connecting with her work.

'I'm not convinced.'

To be fair, neither was she. She looked down at the cool greys and blues, the muted colours and couldn't take offence. She liked elements of the brand-new design, but her core concept remained vague. After days of trying to crack the design, she was creatively stuck. Sharing her half-formed ideas with Judah wasn't confidence—it was a silent plea for direction, for anything he liked that might spark her inspiration and give her direction.

'Sorry, Calla, it's just not me.'

Ugh. She sighed and wrinkled her nose.

He folded his arms across his chest. 'What's the problem?'

Well, since he asked. 'You haven't given me much to work on,' she told him, trying to keep her tone professional. 'You don't have any strong feelings about colours, or a style or finishes. You gave me a few photographs from when you were a kid, but they were photos of you and your parents, not of the house. And you said that you wanted me to capture the vibe, not necessarily the décor.'

Judah frowned. 'I gave you carte blanche.'

What clients didn't realise was that creative freedom wasn't as much fun as people expected it to be. Anything and everything was on the table, and she didn't know what he liked or was even drawn to. And when she asked what he liked about his apartment in London—or flat as he called it—he told her it was decorated per his father's taste, and he hadn't had time to update it. So no help there. But she couldn't ignore the fact that she hadn't pushed him harder, interrogated him about what he wanted in a home, what he liked and hated. Maybe she hadn't *wanted* to ask the tougher questions because it would've meant digging deeper—getting too close. Given their history, digging was emotionally dangerous.

Still, she couldn't play it safe. If she was going to do this properly—if she was going to reclaim her professional reputation and rebuild her business—she had to bite the bullet. She couldn't design a home for a man she was too afraid to understand.

She scowled and blew air into her cheeks. She needed to go back to the drawing board. Literally.

Judah reached into the under-counter fridge, pulled out a beer and offered her one. Shrugging—it was after five—Calla took the drink and slid onto a bar stool tucked beneath the freestanding marble-and-wood island. The outdoor kitchen and bar were far nicer than the actual indoor kitchen; in fact, the whole entertainment area functioned as an outside room. And with its ceiling fans and incredible vista, it was her favourite place to be.

Judah took a pull of his beer and reached back into the fridge to pull out a long fish. 'I caught it earlier while trawling off the kayak,' he explained. 'I was going to grill it for supper. Do you want to join me?'

She should say no, but she didn't want to return to the cool, quiet, but oh-so-empty guest house. But she needed to push her attraction aside, and if she could make this meal about work, maybe she could grill Judah over his design decisions while he cooked and they ate.

Oh, Calla, be honest. You're just looking for an excuse to spend time with him. But who could blame her? In chino shorts, an untucked mint green button-down shirt, cuffs haphazardly rolled back, and bare feet—his nose a little sunburned and his lips chapped, he looked like the surfer-bartender she'd met ten months ago. Seeing him like this, she'd never believe he was the CEO of one of the world's premier wellness companies.

'Are you working at the moment or taking a break?' she asked.

'I wish I could switch off,' he said, pulling a filleting knife from the block behind him, 'but I still had to give the company a couple of pints of blood today.'

'It's that demanding?'

'It's that demanding,' he admitted. 'I always knew I'd be doing this someday. I just thought I'd have more time to prepare.' He brushed a lock of hair off his forehead with the back of his wrist. 'I thought I'd have my dad to guide me while I gained experience.'

Underneath his words, she heard a note of anxiety, even desperation. Was she letting her imagination run wild? She scratched the side of her neck. 'Why do I get the sense that you hate being the CEO?'

He didn't raise his eyes from his task. 'I hate that my dad died. I don't hate that I'm the CEO.'

'I don't believe you.'

Judah laid down his knife and placed his

palms on the counter, the muscles in his forearms tensing. 'Hate…well, *hate* is a strong word. I just feel, I don't know, out of sync—like this is surreal.'

Despite knowing she shouldn't, that she should change the subject back to something, anything, work related, Calla leaned forward, curious for more. 'Talk to me, Judah.'

His intelligent eyes slammed into hers. 'It veers from the professional into the personal, Calla.'

Well, later she couldn't squeal that she hadn't been warned. She nodded. 'Unfortunately, I just realised that, as much as I want to keep our relationship business based, in order to do my job, I'm going to need to get a little personal now and again.' She saw his frown and winced. 'I know, I don't like it either.'

'You're putting words in my mouth again, Calla.' Judah picked up his knife and sliced into the fish. Their eyes caught and his half-smile was gently reassuring and some of the tension in her neck and shoulders eased.

'One of the reasons I came back to St Croix is because I'm looking for something real. Something that makes sense again.' He exhaled, the confession seeming to catch in his throat. He cleared it, but when he spoke, his voice still sounded scratchy. 'The truth is, and as much as you don't want to hear it, the half weekend I spent with you? Well, that was the last time I felt like me. Not the version of myself people expected, not the Reyes heir, the CEO, the largest stockholder of an international company. Just…me.'

He shrugged. 'And I guess I've been chasing that feeling ever since.'

Shock flickered through her, and bright sparks seared her skin. A part of her, the part in charge of protecting herself, wanted to argue—but no words came out. After a couple of beats, she cleared her throat, desperately thinking of something to say.

She didn't understand.

'I'm confused,' she admitted.

'The company was my father's. I never established it or was part of its vision. I've spent the past few months completing projects my father planned and initiated. Nothing I've done since inheriting the company has my stamp on it. I feel like I own it but have no connection to it.'

She could understand that. 'It must've been quite a shock going from being a bartender to a boss.'

He handed her a grim smile and nodded. 'At the time we met, I was working my way through the company, spending time in all the Reyes Luxe departments to get a handle on the business from the ground up. I just happened to be working in the St Croix hotel at the time and was helping out by doing a few shifts behind the bar.'

She leaned forward, fascinated. 'I presume your dad wanted you to learn the business by starting at the bottom.'

He shook his head. 'No. He wanted me in the office next to him, wearing two-thousand-dollar suits, receiving a fat salary and a title I hadn't earned. It was my choice to learn the business from the ground up.'

Her respect for him rose. Most of his peers would've taken the easy route to the top of the food chain.

'So...now that you have the corner office, you're doubting it's where you should be?' she prodded, fascinated by this glimpse into his psyche. He came across as so stoic and unflappable, but beneath his calm surface churned a wide, silent whirlpool.

'I don't have the luxury of doubt. I have to suck it up and make it work,' he muttered. 'My biggest challenge is where do we go from here?' Judah flipped the fish over to fillet the other side. 'The Reyes Luxe board, and my executives, have many ideas on where they want the company to go, what they want to do with it, and how to expand our footprint. I get a hundred ideas a day, none of which I connect with.'

'Can you give me an example?' Calla asked.

'Well, everyone thinks I should acquire Forge-Ritual, a male-slanted wellness company. I'm not sold on the brand.'

'Why not?'

'It leans into promoting machismo, and I think even a whiff of hyper-masculinity can be toxic. I don't believe anyone should dictate what masculinity should look like in the twenty-first century. Everyone around me disagrees with me, mostly because acquiring the company would be very good for the company's bottom line.'

Calla bit the inside of her cheek. 'Can I state the obvious and say that you should follow your gut?'

He released a small snort. 'My gut and I have stopped communicating, mostly because the past ten months have been crazy, and utterly surreal. I feel like an actor who has been shoved into a play and hasn't had time to read the script. I badly need a reset, to recalibrate, and I thought being back here in St Croix was a good way to do it.'

There was more of the iceberg to uncover, but she wasn't going to push him. He'd already given her so much more than she'd expected. And by opening this door, treating him as a client was going to be so much harder. And all her fault.

'I'm sorry, Judah.'

He managed a small smile. 'It is what it is.' He hooked his finger around the neck of his beer bottle and lifted it to his lips, his eyes on Buck Island. 'But working from Sol House is much nicer than working from the company HQ in London or at our offices in New York or Singapore.'

She looked around, took in the playful sea. 'It's not too shabby,' she agreed, tongue in cheek.

'Is this where you feel completely comfortable?' she asked, tapping her index finger against the neck of her beer bottle. 'Relaxed and utterly at home?'

'There's only ever been one other place where I've enjoyed as much.'

She leaned forward, intrigued. Another island? A city? 'Where?'

His hands stilled, and he looked up, transferring his attention from the fish to her. His eyes were a fire blue, a small smile played on his lips and she sensed his answer before he spoke. 'When I walked into my friend's surfside shack with you, I felt instantly at home,' he murmured.

Calla did her best to ignore the heat in her veins, her suddenly erratic heartbeat. She tipped her head to the side, intrigued. 'Is it still around?' she asked.

Judah shook his head. 'No. Sadly, it was destroyed in a hurricane last season,' he replied.

Calla thought back, trying to push aside memories of Judah taking off his shirt, the way he kissed her, held her, unable to recollect what the shack looked like. She'd barely taken her eyes off Judah, and little about the seaside shack, except for the way the light streamed in through the sea-facing windows onto his spectacular body, registered.

'I don't remember much. Can you describe it for me?' she asked, placing her chin in the palm of her hand. She was only asking because it might inspire some design ideas. Yeah, and a purple pig just flew across the endlessly blue sky.

'It was a cluttered mess,' he told her, smiling. 'Surfboards lined the walls, the floor was concrete and paint-splattered and it had been used as a painting studio by the previous tenant. The couch was huge. I was able to stretch out on it, battered but so damn comfortable. The bed was against the back wall…'

Yes, she remembered the bed. She swallowed and played with the silver bangle on her wrist. 'Colour scheme?' she asked.

'Mostly white, hints of blue. The artists left an abstract mural in bold pink and orange on one wall.'

'I remember that mural—it was amazing. Depending on how the light caught it, it was bold and brilliant, a Caribbean sunset, or muted and lovely, a gentle sunrise. How could I have forgotten?'

Because remembering one thing meant unlocking all the rest, and that would've left her aching for an impossible *something.* Unlocking one memory led to others—his hot skin over hard muscle, the way he said her name like it was something precious, the reverence in his touch. His clever mouth painting kisses across her belly, over her hip, his hands streaking down her thighs with an urgency that made her feel worshipped and wanted.

The warmth in his eyes, the way he looked at her like she held all the secrets to the universe. Like she was enough. Like she *mattered.*

It was too much; he was too much. Needing to regain her equilibrium, Calla slid off her seat and walked over to the opposite wall, her eyes taking in the twenty-plus framed photographs on the wall. Some were from the past five or ten years—there were a couple of Judah and his dad holding surfboards and standing on paddleboards, in a restaurant—but others were of a young Judah and a stunning-looking woman with the same eyes and shape face. She tapped the woman's face. 'Your mum?'

Judah looked up. 'Mm. The super-cute kid with her is me.'

'It's a pity you grew up to be ugly,' she quipped, relieved when Judah smiled at her joke. She was out of practice and had forgotten how to gently tease. Had she ever teased Jack? No, she'd never felt comfortable enough.

Calla returned her attention to the photographs. The last photo of Judah and his mum together was when he was around ten or so. 'Did she die?' He nodded.

Calla winced. 'When?'

'When I was eleven.' He wrapped the fish in foil, paying the fish far more attention than it deserved. 'She was diagnosed with pancreatic cancer in March and was gone by July.' He walked over to the sink to wash his hands, and Calla watched his profile as he looked out at the sunset gathering its colours on the horizon. 'It was a grim time.'

She could imagine. She'd lost her only parent, her dad, in her late teens—her mum took off when she was a baby—and she still missed her father so much. She couldn't pull her eyes off another photo of Judah, and his mum and dad. They looked so happy, a complete unit. Her dad had been her person, all she'd ever needed and she fell apart when he died. Was it her desperation to belong, for a family, that made her leap at the chance to join the Abernathy clan? Maybe. She'd never thought about it like that before; it was something to unpack. She looked at the next photo, one of Judah and his dad, looking so similar, laughing. 'You and your dad look close,' she commented.

He turned to face her, drying his hands with a kitchen towel. 'We had a couple of rough years after Mum died, and he didn't spend much time at home. But we got closer when I got older. Spending weeks here every summer helped. He taught me to surf, to paddleboard.'

Judah asked her to open a bottle of white wine. After pulling the cork, Calla resumed her seat and tipped Chardonnay into their glasses. She'd veered off course, leaving the professional behind and heading into personal; but in this particular tug-o-war, curiosity kicked caution's butt. Besides, asking a few questions didn't have to mean anything. It wasn't a sign she was losing control. It couldn't be. There was no reason they couldn't be friends.

And the more she understood him—what made him tick, what resonated with him, the memories he held on to—the better she'd be able to shape Sol House into something that felt like his. Well, that was what she was telling herself, *begging* herself to believe. 'I'm sorry you lost him, Judah.'

Judah pulled salad ingredients from the fridge and reached for a platter.

'Yeah, it was a shock. One moment I was doing shifts as a Reyes Luxe bartender, learning the ropes, the next I was the boss of bosses.' He shrugged and leaned his hip into the counter, the salad forgotten. 'It was such a crazy time,' he admitted, his voice low. 'I had to arrange his funeral, fly back to the UK, meet with lawyers and board members, wrap my head around the fact that, as the major shareholder of Reyes Luxe, I was expected to, per my dad's wishes, run the company.'

Calla bit the corner of her lip. 'Did you have time to grieve him?' she softly asked.

Judah lifted one shoulder. 'I don't know. The first three months were a blur, the second three not much better. In a way, I still feel like I'm on autopilot, just following the blueprint my dad left for me.'

Calla placed her wine glass on the island and snagged a baby tomato destined for their salad. 'What do you mean by that?' Judah took a while to respond, and she knew he was debating how much to tell her. She waited, expecting him to deflect or steer the conversation somewhere safer—toward her designs for the house or logistics or the weather. That's what she would've done, what she always did when someone asked for more of her than she was willing to give. Vulnerability was too big a risk. She either deflected the conversation or threw up walls—along with being a good designer, she was a master builder of emotional walls.

'As the new face and voice of Reyes Luxe, I became very newsworthy very quickly, and that was difficult, for many reasons. I was this golden heir, portrayed as someone who had a great education, wealth and decent looks.' Calling his looks 'decent' was like calling an iceberg an ice cube. 'Everyone quickly forgot I was in this position because I'd lost my father.'

Right. When she thought about it that way, it cast his grief in a different light.

'And God, it's such a pain in the arse being the "face" of a wellness empire,' he said, pulling a face. 'If I look tired, and I often look tired because I suffer from insomnia, our range of vitamins don't work. If I'm not seen at my regular gym, I'm either sick or lazy. If I talk to a woman, even casually, we're dating.'

That was the problem with being young, gorgeous and eligible. And carrying the name of a fitness, wellness and nutrition empire. 'All I want to do is once, just once, walk down a street eating chocolate-drenched ice cream.'

'Do you like ice cream?'

Judah smiled, and it felt like the sun had slipped out from behind a heavy cloud to shine on her. 'I bloody love ice cream. And chocolate. And anything able to give me cavities.'

She couldn't help it, she laughed. Judah smiled at her, and Calla placed her fist into her sternum, feeling the warm glow in her stomach, the boom-boom of her heart. Just like before, this man could make her feel, make her laugh and crack her façade.

'My dad had been vociferously against anything containing sugar. He'd hated anything sweet, including honey and xylitol so when my friends were sneaking weed and beer into their houses, I was sneaking in chocolate bars and tubs of ice cream. I still make furtive late-night runs to the store and then pay for it the next morning by adding thirty minutes to my gym workout.' He saw the question on her face and grinned. 'And yes, it's always worth it.'

Calla gave him a long up-and-down look. 'The occasional ice cream binge hasn't hurt you, though,' she told him. 'You look fitter, harder, than you were before.'

'Have you been checking me out, Calla?' he teased, blue eyes glinting.

Calla waved her hand, knocked her wine glass, and she just managed to catch it before it tipped over. She sucked wine off her hand and wrinkled her nose at the drops on her shorts. Judah handed her a kitchen towel, and she wiped the counter, desperately hoping for a sea breeze to cool her face.

Judah leaned his hip against the counter, folded his arms and his sexy biceps bulged. 'Technically, I work out for the sake of my employees.'

Calla tilted her head. 'How so?'

He nodded, straight-faced. 'If I don't exercise, I get cranky. Nobody wants a cranky boss. Basically, my abs contribute to my employees' mental health.'

She snorted, trying to hide her amusement. 'Wow, your generosity knows no bounds. But are you sure they are as sexy as you think they are?'

With complete confidence, he lifted his shirt. His shorts hung low on his hips, and her fingers itched to dance over his stomach's defined ridges. She released a loud sigh, and Judah bowed.

Calla's laugh burst out before she could stop it, and heat rushed to her cheeks. 'God, you are insufferable!'

He leaned, just a little, enough for her to smell his sexy sea-and-spice scent. 'You're blushing, West.'

Of course she was—a sexy, younger man was flirting with her. And she was loving it. Not that she'd let him know that. She pointed her wine glass at him. 'You're imagining things.'

Those blue eyes glinted with mischief. ‘Maybe. But I’m not the one knocking over wine glasses.’

Calla rolled her eyes and took a sip. ‘Be careful when you walk back into the house, Reyes. I’m not sure the big rooms and high ceilings are expansive enough to accommodate your enormous ego.’

Judah chuckled and clinked his glass gently against hers before returning to assembling the salad. ‘Let’s eat, I’m starving.’

Calla wasn’t sure whether she was relieved or sad that he’d changed the subject and ended their brief bout of flirting. Their attraction still flickered between them—light, flirty and dangerous.

She picked up her glass again and took a deliberate sip, breathing deeply.

How was she ever going to put their relationship back on a professional footing? Did she even want to?

Later that evening, Calla sat beside Judah, their feet dangling in the warm water of the pool, glasses of red wine resting on the tiles behind them. The air was thick with humidity but fragrant, carrying notes of jasmine and sea brine. The rhythmic chorus of tree frogs competed with the soft jazz drifting from hidden speakers.

It was a stunning night—warm and still. And

she'd had a lovely, unpressured evening. She and Judah had caught up, silently agreeing to keep their conversation light and nonconfrontational as they'd eaten his fried fish and salad. The meal ended with simple bowls of vanilla ice cream. Judah's portion, naturally, had been three times the size of hers.

She circled back to their earlier conversation, picking it apart. One question still lingered—one Judah had carefully avoided answering.

'Why aren't you sleeping?' she softly asked.

She looked at his profile and sensed his tension.

'I employ over ten thousand people across six countries. I own gyms, spas, meditation centres and professional sports facilities. I have a life coaching franchise, a vitamin line and a mindfulness and wellness app. I've got a lot on my plate and it keeps me awake.'

It sounded a lot, *was* a lot, but Calla knew he was capable of juggling the demands of a huge company. He had an excellent degree and was whip-smart. His inability to sleep went deeper than his day-to-day work pressures. 'And I'm pretty sure you could do all that with your eyes closed,' she told him. 'What's the real reason?'

Judah's eyes slammed into hers. 'You're pretty curious for someone who never talks about herself.'

Calla lifted one shoulder. Being emotionally isolated was the only way she could protect herself from being emotionally battered again. She didn't have anyone to stand between her and the world and could only rely on herself. So she had to be her own advocate and protector. It was a matter of survival.

Understanding the power of silence to get people to talk, Calla simply waited. Maybe he'd talk to her, maybe he wouldn't. She couldn't force him. Nobody, she suspected, could force Judah Reyes to do anything he didn't want to do.

Judah gripped the edge of the pool. 'Since he died, I've been following my father's vision for the company. I've completed projects he started, finalised deals he negotiated, bought and sold assets and melded companies as per his five-year plan. He died in the middle of it, so I've done my best to complete it.'

Calla had no doubt he'd done everything required of him. He'd fulfilled his dad's wishes. What more could be asked of him? 'So what's the problem?'

Judah twisted his lips. 'The problem is that I need to figure out *my* five-year plan, work out where I want to take this company, and what my vision for the company is. I don't have a blueprint to follow anymore. How much do I want to carry over from the past? What do I want to do that's new?' He hesitated, looked down at his hands. 'What's authentic?'

He'd used that word before, and it seemed to carry more weight with him than the rest.

'Does it not feel like it is?' she asked.

Agitation had him kicking his foot, making the pool water ripple. Knowing how rock-steady he always was, the calmest port in a storm, she knew she'd touched a nerve.

'I don't know how to answer that. Or, rather, I don't *want* to answer your question. Because if I say no, then I'm invalidating my father's work, work he was immensely proud of. If I say yes, then I'll be lying to myself and you.'

'So it's a little of both?'

'It's a *lot* of both. I need to plot a way forward, and I know it's not going to be the same way as my dad's. I feel guilty about that, because he put in thirty years of slogging to get Reyes Luxe the way it is. What right do I have to change it?'

He stared in the direction of Buck's Island. 'But if I do change it, what do I change it to? What feels right to me? What can I live with?'

Judah's words hit a little too close to home.

For ten months, she'd thrown herself into salvaging her career without ever asking why. Watching Judah struggle with a legacy he hadn't chosen, she saw herself—lost, uncertain, maybe chasing something out of habit or pride.

Was she rebuilding to prove something to herself? Or was it just an exhausting *up yours* to Jack and everyone who believed him?

Did she really, truly still want this career—or had she simply forgotten how to want anything else?

But this wasn't about her; it was about him.

He was torn between what felt right and what he felt he owed his dad. What he should keep, and what he should let go of. Where he could make his mark. And how to do it. Because he was so steady, so thinking, and so very confident, she frequently forgot he was still young, only thirty-two. He still had so much time. He was putting more pressure on himself than he needed to, but Calla knew he would not appreciate her saying so.

But how could she help him? What could she say? 'When last did you feel truly authentic? Like you were fully and utterly yourself?' she asked.

Judah's head snapped up, and his eyes slammed into hers. His gaze intensified, and his eyes turned to lasers, slicing through her carefully constructed walls, looking deep into her soul. He surprised her when he dropped into the pool fully clothed and, because he stood in the shallow end, she could look directly into his eyes. He placed his hands on the warm tiles on either side of her hips, effectively caging her in. In the warm glow of the underwater pool lights, she clocked the flickers of deep gold in his eyes, his stubby dark eyelashes, the scar running along his jaw. The scent of him, olive oil and sea, spice and citrus, made her feel a little swoony, and her nipples tightened. The space between her legs heated, and her womb throbbed.

He was the only man, ever, who could shut down her brain and stop her synapses firing, who could transport her to bed with one look. God, if he kissed her, she would be in serious trouble.

It was trouble she didn't need. But it was also the trouble she craved.

Judah lowered his head, and his lips whispered along her cheek bone, down to her jaw and the side of her mouth. His lips slid across hers, light, feathery, and Calla had to clench her fists to keep from reaching for him, from sliding her hands up and under his shirt to find ripped muscles under his tanned, hot skin. She wanted him. For the first time in months, the first time since him, she wanted to be horizontal and naked with him.

Any type of naked with him.

'I answered your question earlier, Calla,' he whispered, his soft breath and his words hitting her ear.

Had he? He was so close, and her need was so great that she couldn't remember what he'd said. Or what she'd asked. 'What were we talking about again?' she asked, a little breathlessly. She wished she could act cooler, be more sophisticated, but she'd only had two lovers in her life, one a lot better than the other.

She didn't know how to play the game. Never had.

He didn't answer her, but instead covered her lips with his clever mouth, and Calla felt herself dissolving, fully immersed in his kiss. He didn't move his hands off the tiles, didn't do anything but kiss her, softly, reverently, like he was rediscovering a previously lost, longed-for land. It was a kiss full of soul, of secrets, hot and sweet and far more seductive than she'd expected.

And it was over far sooner than she wanted. Or expected.

Judah pulled back. 'The last time I felt truly authentic was with you, Calla. In that surf shack last year. I'll keep reminding you until my words sink in.'

Oh.

Oh...

Calla went still, every muscle contracting, as reality rolled over her. She couldn't afford to let his words sink in, to let them resonate. Honesty was his weapon, and it always left her vulnerable. So she did what she was good at—what kept her safe. Her hands slid up to his shoulders, her palms flat against the hard muscles of his chest. Then she pushed.

And when he stumbled back a step, she scrambled up and ran.

CHAPTER SIX

SHE'D RUN OFF. Again.

Judah linked his hands behind his head and released a long sigh as he watched Calla's slim frame move across the entertainment area, her body tight with tension, leaving wet footprints behind. She didn't glance back but just skipped down the stairs to the garden like she needed to get as far away from him as quickly as possible.

After hauling himself out of the pool, he walked over to the wall, looked down and watched as she hit the path bisecting the manicured lawn, moving quickly across the stone pavers. She pulled open the door to the guest house and disappeared from view.

She was very good at shutting him out. Mentally and physically.

It happened every time he got too close or too real, when she clocked his desire for her or when their heat became too much to ignore. The second he showed her that his attraction hadn't faded—not even close—or that she might feel thc same, she hit Eject without a moment's hesitation.

He gripped the wall with both hands and allowed his head to drop. The taste of her was still on his tongue, and he could sense her breath on his lips. That kiss—God, that kiss. He couldn't call it a mistake, nor was it something he could regret. Touching her was both a pleasure and a privilege. She'd responded, and for too brief a moment, she'd fallen into him. Her lips moved against his, soft and sexy. He'd definitely felt her body soften, lean, give in to the madness flaming between them.

But then she'd remembered who she was. And why she was here and what was at stake. Then she'd stiffened and pulled back. And bolted.

He knew what she was doing right now, and that was pacing the guest house, mentally composing a list of reasons why she was right to shut down their kiss, to keep things between them professional. To keep their fire contained and controlled.

Frustration flared, and Judah dropped a series of F-bombs. He could've deepened the kiss, taken more, and she might've—would've—followed. But he didn't want her like that. Oblivious, and carried away. When they came back together, he wanted her to make a deliberate choice to be with him, to take what he offered, to enjoy the heat and the flames. He didn't want her off balance and resentful after they'd slept together.

He knew she'd been through something—maybe many somethings—both during her marriage and in the months since he'd last seen her. She didn't need to explain; the signs were everywhere. It was obvious that money had been tight; he saw it in the outdated phone she used, in the too-slow laptop with the crack in the corner of the screen. He presumed every cent went back into her business. She'd told him she needed this job, but he instinctively knew there was more than money on the line.

He scrubbed his hands over his face. He understood her need to keep their relationship on a business footing. The power dynamic between them was unequal and firmly tipped to benefit him. She needed to keep him happy, professionally, and didn't want to mess up her chances of future work by muddying the waters with a sexual affair. Calla was smart to be wary, and, understandably, didn't want their attraction to taint her work. She wanted to earn it. On her own merit. And, damn it, she deserved to.

The problem was now that he'd touched her again, he didn't know how he was supposed to keep from doing it. They were back where it all started, and the island held so many memories of her, memories he was desperate to revisit. Did they ambush her too? Did she remember the way they'd kissed like people did after dicing death? Rolling together in the surf, sand sticking to their skin? Teaching her to surf and how she'd laughed every time she fell? Undressing each other in the moonlight? So little time, but chock-full of moments.

That weekend was burned into him. It was the happiest, most uncomplicated stretch of time he could remember. Was it any wonder he wanted to re-create it?

But what if he was still on the first page and she'd finished the book and had moved on?

What then?

Frustrated, Calla threw down her pencil and scowled at the bright pink paddleboard making its way across Solitude Bay, skimming the surface of the calm, stunning sea. Why couldn't she transfer the fleeting images flashing across her mind onto the empty page of her sketchbook in front of her? This had never happened to her before, and there seemed to be a block between her mind and the blank page in front of her. She'd been here for ten days now, and she'd accomplished nothing.

Was Judah *that* big a distraction? Was her mind so full of him that she couldn't concentrate on anything else? Or was she so worried about her business and her career, her future, that she'd created a mental block? Calla pulled her feet up onto the seat of her chair and wrapped her arms around her knees. Being in Judah's arms last night, feeling his lips on her mouth, had been pure heaven. She'd felt both intoxicated and protected, safe and turned on. How could he pull so many emotions to the surface at the same time?

This was exactly why mixing business with pleasure was a terrible idea. Romance in the workplace was a minefield—messy, distracting and full of regret. Sex blurred boundaries, scrambled one's focus and made people forget the damn job. How was she supposed to concentrate when the GPS in her brain kept rerouting to imagining Judah naked—in the shower, in her bed, pressed up against her, touching and kissing her like it was the only way to keep the world turning? *Argh!*

'What did the sea do to you?'

Calla looked up to see Judah standing at the edge of the veranda, dressed in board shorts and nothing else, sunlight bouncing off his tanned, bare chest. The light hair on his chest was more golden than she remembered, and his abs more defined. His board shorts hung low on his hips and showed off sexy hip muscles.

'Calla?'

Calla tapped the side of her head with the heel of her palm to kick-start her brain. Right. What had he asked? She looked down at her sketchpad. 'I'm frustrated because I can't seem to translate my vision to paper.' She scowled at the empty page.

Judah held the point of his gleaming white surfboard. 'Maybe you need a break, to step away for a while. Why don't you come to the beach with me?'

Calla shook her head. She was already working in shorts and flip-flops, and at a dining table outside instead of a desk. Her standards were slipping, and she couldn't play hooky either. 'Judah, I'm already so far behind it's not even funny. You wanted an initial proposal in two weeks—that's three days away, and I don't know how I'm going to make that deadline.'

'So do you think it will help to sit there and force your brain to cooperate?' he asked. Calla was glad he didn't say something asinine like 'I'll extend your deadline' or 'take your time'. Statements like that would've been an insult. She was a professional, dammit.

'Well?' he asked, raising his eyebrow when she didn't answer his question.

'No, I'll probably just get more frustrated and more annoyed,' she admitted. 'But that doesn't mean I should go to the beach instead.'

'Take some time off, Calla, make up for it later.' His mouth lifted in that sexy half-smile, half smirk she adored. 'Nobody is going to report you to the productivity police.'

Calla wrinkled her nose. It wasn't that. Or only that. She didn't think that spending non-working time, especially when they were half naked, with Judah was a good idea. Their chemistry was constantly bubbling, ready to ignite. One touch, one kiss, and she suspected they might self-immolate. They should be keeping their distance, not trying to find ways to spend more time together.

'The sun is shining, and the sea is warm,' Judah coaxed. 'Get your pretty butt out of the chair and go change into a bikini.'

'I'm thirty-eight years old, I think I'm far too old for a bikini,' she whipped back.

'Sweetheart, that body was made to be shown off,' he drawled, igniting baby fireworks on her skin. 'Besides, you made that stupid rule? If you feel confident in a bikini, no matter your age, wear whatever the hell you want.'

He had a way of cutting through to the heart of what was important, of clearing away the extraneous and finding the simple truth. In so many ways, she had a lot to learn from him. Calla placed her pencil in her case, closed her sketch pad and pushed back her chair. She sent Judah a quick glance and sighed.

From the moment he uttered his invitation, she knew she was going to join him, that she would say yes. Oh, she could B.S. herself, throw up a couple of mental roadblocks to make herself feel better, and more in control. Did she want to recapture some of the feelings from those heady days she spent with him last year? To feel the way she did back then? That would be a solid, hell, yes!

She should work. She wasn't going to. And if that meant a sleepless night wrestling with her creativity, then that was the price she'd pay.

'Shall I meet you out front?' she asked.

Judah nodded and loosely held his surfboard against his side. 'Sounds good. Ten minutes?'

Calla nodded, caught by the intense expression on his face. She waited, knowing he had more to say. 'But Calla...if you come to the beach with me, you come as you. Not as my interior decorator. As you.'

She heard his unspoken words...*as the woman you were back then.* She leaned back in her chair and watched him walk away, big, solid, in control. She knew she should stay put, knew she was taking a risk, but he was the only man who could tempt her into exploring life at the end of her comfort zone, like she was standing at the end of a cliff. There was a good chance that she would fall, end up emotionally splattered on the rocks below, but the urge to recapture those sunshine- and laughter-filled days, when the world stopped and only the two of them existed, was too tempting to resist.

Don't cry later, Calla. You knew what you were getting into. So don't you dare cry.

Judah held his surfboard under his arm, a backpack on his back and a cooler in his other hand. He picked his way through the rocks and turned back to look at Calla, scrambling over a boulder behind him. She wore black board shorts over a lime and pink bikini, her hair bundled up under a black baseball cap. Her sunglasses kept slipping down her nose and her towel kept falling off her slim shoulder. She looked like she was in her early twenties.

Her age had never been an issue for him, and he thought it a stupid barrier people threw up to avoid getting hurt. Who cared if she was six years older? To him, it wouldn't matter if she was ten or even fifteen years older; he just… liked her. Always had. Attraction and connection didn't stop to ask for birth dates or age differences, it just looked at the other person and said 'yep, her'.

Besides, if the situation were reversed and he

were older, nobody would blink. And that was hypocrisy at its finest. Sometimes, in certain situations and at certain times, others would immediately ascertain that she was older than him; at other times, like now, they'd assume she was younger or, at the very least, the same age as him. The thing was, it didn't bloody matter. It never would.

'How much longer?' Calla called, and Judah grinned at the hint of a whine in her voice.

'You should exercise more and eat better,' he replied, ducking his head to hide his smile.

'Oh, shut up,' Calla shot back. 'I walk when I can.'

'But I bet you grab ready-made meals, slices of pizza and Chinese when you are in a hurry.'

'Not always Chinese. I try to keep things balanced by eating Thai, Korean and Vietnamese food, too,' she whipped back.

'My point is that you should be cooking for yourself more, eating fresh vegetables you've prepared yourself.'

'Like you do?' she asked, jumping off a rock onto the beach. She immediately kicked off her flip-flops and dug her toes into the sand, closing her eyes as she found joy in the simple pleasure. 'You probs have a chef or a housekeeper who leaves perfect meals in the fridge for you.

I don't. Besides, when would I have the time to cook? I work fourteen-plus hours.'

He didn't like the idea of her working so hard for so little return. 'I'm just saying, you need to look after yourself better.'

Calla patted his bare shoulder, sending waves of electricity through his system. He was acting like he was thirteen, and it was the first time a girl had touched him. What was wrong with him? Oh, nothing, except the woman he'd dreamed of for the better part of a year was standing in front of him, half dressed, looking gorgeous with a small, sexy smile on her lovely face.

'Stop nagging me about my eating and exercising habits, Reyes,' she told him, skipping ahead of him. 'I'm taking a few hours off from real life. And in the little bubble I'm creating, there are no calories, sun doesn't cause cancer and stress doesn't exist.' She dropped her beach bag and planted her pretty butt in the sand and bent her shapely legs.

She looked around. 'The beach is empty,' she stated, sounding satisfied.

'It's one the locals use,' he explained. 'It'll get busy later.'

She smiled up at him, and Judah was sure his heart stopped beating. He dropped to balance on his haunches in front of her. She'd opened the door, and he was a fool not to walk right in. He stroked the back of her cheek, then her jaw, with his knuckle. 'In this bubble you've created, can we roll back time and be the two people we were back then?'

She stared at him, her eyes wide. But she didn't say no, so he pushed the rim of her cap to the back of her head and lowered his mouth to hers, picking up where they last left off with a hot, demanding open-mouthed kiss. Calla stiffened, for just a heartbeat, second thoughts nipping, but then she lifted her hand to touch his jaw, to run her fingers down his neck, over his shoulder. He ravaged her mouth, and her tongue joined him in that age-old dance. This... God, *this* was what he needed.

Hauling her to her feet, he banded his arm around her waist and lifted her to her toes, and her arms tightened around his neck. A hand under her butt boosted her up his body, and her legs wrapped his hips, her feminine core against his hard, need-her-now erection. Her mouth tasted of mint and coffee, and he couldn't remember when last he felt so alive, so utterly lost in the moment.

Judah walked her towards the ocean, his mouth not leaving hers. The warm water hit his ankles, then his calves, then his thighs. Calla, lost in their kiss, didn't react when the water soaked her shorts and lapped her waist. Their kiss was so hot that Judah was surprised steam didn't rise off the water. Calla crossed her ankles behind his back and clenched her thigh muscles, her expression blissful. She tipped her head to the side, and he scraped his teeth along the cords of her neck, over her collarbone and shoulder. Using one fingertip, he pushed the strap of her bikini down her arm to nip at the ball of her shoulder, loving her soft and smooth lime-scented skin. Pulling back to look at her, Judah smiled at her closed eyes, her parted, slick lips. She looked relaxed and turned-on, lost in this moment.

He couldn't resist seeing more of her, so he pulled the cup of her bikini top down, his eyes feasting on her budded nipple, softly pink in the sunlight. Ducking his head, he pulled it into his mouth, flattening it against the roof of his mouth with his tongue. Calla arched her back, her fingers spearing his hair, making those sexy sounds of want and need.

He liked her like this, loose and letting go.

Talking of letting go…

While this beach was currently empty, it wasn't private, and if someone should come along, he'd give them a show. He had to stop now, before they went too far. Reluctantly, he released her and, in one swift movement, pulled her bikini back into place. Burying his head in her neck, he closed his eyes, trying to push back the wave of desire threatening to buckle his knees. He was a good sailor, a better surfer, had spearfished and spent a good portion of his life on the ocean, and very little scared him. But Calla was on another level. She, on so many levels, exhilarated and terrified him.

Calla's legs dropped from his hips, and she found her footing, her feet digging into the sea floor. She tried to pull away, but there was no way he was going to let that happen, so he pulled her to him, turning her so that her back was to his chest, his arms criss-crossing her torso, his still-hard erection pressing into her back. 'No, don't pull away,' he said in her ear. 'I stopped kissing you because this isn't a private beach and I don't want you to be embarrassed.'

She relaxed and sagged, just a little, against him. He raked back her hair with wet fingers. 'I've imagined kissing you so many times, but it was a million times better than I imagined,' he murmured.

'Maybe you have a really terrible imagination,' she said, her voice a little shaky.

That wasn't possible. 'Better,' he insisted.

Calla gripped his forearm, her fingernails digging into his skin. 'What do we do now, Judah? How do we go forward?'

She was someone who needed a plan, a way forward, preferably signposted. 'We swim, I surf, we lie in the sun and eat,' he said, keeping it simple. 'We chat.'

She sighed. 'I don't know what we have to talk about,' she said.

'We both know that we could talk for days, years, and not run out of things to say, Calla,' he replied, striving for patience. She was scared, he could feel it vibrating through her, knew it like he knew his signature. Scared of what she was feeling, the passion between them, mixing business and pleasure, her future. But he'd do anything he could to make her fear go away.

And if that meant giving her the damn contract to revamp his house, he would. She could mess up his house, paint the walls lemon green and the skirtings pink, cover the couches with flamingo or leopard prints and he wouldn't say a damn word. Not that he thought, for one moment, she'd screw up that badly. But he'd sacrifice his house to give her a little financial breathing room.

Not that she'd accept any charity from him.

'I'm not very good at compartmentalising, Judah.'

He nuzzled his nose into her hair, kissed her temple. 'Try it for the next three hours, Cal. Just one hundred and eighty minutes.'

He felt her stiffen, knew she was thinking too much and would talk her way off this beach and back to work. There was no way he was going to let that happen. So he placed his hand on top of her head and, as she opened her mouth to talk, pushed her head under an incoming wave.

Lying back on her elbows on a huge beach blanket, Calla tipped her face up to the sun and closed her eyes. She'd needed this, needed the sea and the sun and the way it made her skin prickle. Or was being with Judah what she needed? Maybe both?

She adjusted her bikini top, which had the tendency to slide to the side, and watched Judah rustle in the cooler box, looking for more to eat. They'd already demolished a couple of sandwiches, some johnnycakes and fresh mango slices. How could he still be hungry?

Calla felt a cold can against her shoulder, and she saw the can of beer Judah offered her. She couldn't manage another bite of food, but she could murder a beer. Sitting up, she took the can, thanked Judah and clinked it against his before taking a long, refreshing sip. There was something amazingly wonderful about downing a cold beer in the hot sun, the ocean just a few feet away.

She squinted at the foot-high waves. 'You're

not going to get any surfing done today,' she told him.

Judah echoed her previous position and leaned back, his elbows taking his weight. He didn't look worried. 'Surfing is a lot better in the winter months. I'm happy to just sit here.'

Calla picked up a handful of sand and allowed it to fall through her clenched fist. St Croix in late June was hot, hot, hot, hot, and she could see a thunderstorm building up on the horizon. She hadn't checked her weather app today and didn't know how intense the storm would be. 'We're not expecting anything crazy weather-wise, right?' she asked.

'Nothing but an afternoon storm. No cyclones or tropical storms are expected anytime soon.'

That was a relief.

'Why do you hate storms so much, Calla?' Judah asked.

She'd been expecting the question, but now that he'd voiced it, she couldn't remember the pat answer she'd normally handed out. Besides, she didn't want to lie to Judah. 'A couple of bad things happened to me during thunderstorms,' she quietly told him.

'Like?'

'Well, the night my dad died, there was the most incredible thunderstorm, with lightning and thunder that was loud and intense.'

'Worse than the other night?' he asked, sitting up and resting his forearms on his bent knees.

She nodded. 'Yeah, worse. He died as the storm petered out.'

He placed his hand on her thigh and squeezed, a quick gesture of support. 'Anything else?'

Unfortunately, there was. 'My ex ended our nearly decade-long marriage during a thunderstorm. But before that, about two years after we got married, I came home after finishing a job early in Washington, DC. I wasn't due home until a few days later. But I missed my husband, and I wanted to surprise him. It was storming when I arrived home, and I didn't have an umbrella with me. I got soaked running from the taxi to the front door, but I was planning on luring him into the shower with me when I got into our apartment.' Judah's dark expression suggested that he knew what was coming next, but she kept talking.

'You caught him.'

She wrinkled her nose. 'No, our place was empty.' She looped her arms around her knees. 'After I showered, I emptied the room's small bin, and while I was tying the bag, I saw an empty lipstick box. High-end, not my colour or my brand.'

Judah's eyes darkened in anger, and his jaw

and fist tightened. He wasn't angry at her, but for her. A novel, slightly weird situation.

'Why didn't you leave him then?' Judah demanded. 'Why did you stay with him? Why did you let him do that to you?'

It was a question she'd asked of herself so many times and in so many ways. She drew her finger in the sand and frowned. The squiggles made no sense. 'While I knew he'd cheated on me, I couldn't toss away everything we had built on such flimsy evidence. We had a business together, and I couldn't walk away from it. I'd given it my everything. We had joint accounts, projects we were working on, he needed me, and I, sure as hell, needed him,' she explained. And Jack had been her *family.* It had been small, dysfunctional, but hers and that was a reason why she'd stayed so much longer than she should've. 'Would you think less of me if I told you that it was easier to push it aside, to ignore it, than to make a big deal of it?'

'It *was* a big deal,' he insisted.

Of course it was. But how could she make him understand? 'Jack was the only person I had in my life, Judah. I never knew my mum, my dad was gone, and I was an only child. I didn't have any extended family and because I worked such long hours, I didn't have any friends. He was my person. I didn't think I could live without him.'

'You were wrong,' he muttered, sounding annoyed.

'I was wrong,' she admitted. 'But it took me a while to realise that, and to realise I'm fine on my own. That I can take care of myself. Honestly, if I can survive being married to and divorcing Jack, I can pretty much survive anything.'

'Was it brutal?'

Brutal? What a tame word for what he put her through! 'He froze me out of the company we created, badmouthed me to our clients, destroyed my reputation and moved money out of our business accounts. Embezzled money from me.' Yeah, it had been brutal. Jack hurt her in every way he possibly could.

She recalled the text message she'd received from him that very morning, and his demand to know when she was returning to the city, and why she was staying so long in St Croix. For some reason, Jack still wasn't done with her and was unable to let her go. He still needed to punish her, to control her, to use her as his verbal punching bag.

But that weekend last year with Judah had been the turning point. It was when she realised that she didn't have to play by Jack's rules anymore, and was reminded, by Judah, that men could be kind. Judah hadn't demanded anything from her. He hadn't pushed or pried—just sat beside her in quiet companionship, letting her breathe. Letting her be.

Back then, she'd told Judah more about herself than she'd shared with anyone in years. Her job. Her past. Her life in New York. What she loved. What she missed. She hadn't mentioned Jack at all.

And when he made love to her as the dawn kissed the sea, she didn't hesitate to follow where he led. Loving him, being with him made perfect sense. Just like it did now.

The urge to kiss him, to run her hands over his perfect body, was almost overwhelming. How far was it to his open-top Jeep? How long would it take them to head back to his house and his bed?

Or any horizontal surface.

Calla sighed, forcing herself to be sensible. They now had ties that bound them, contracts and money on the line, and future projects to consider. They weren't two random strangers who could shed their clothes and inhibitions, believing they'd never see each other again. This was real, grown-up, far-reaching. She had to tread carefully. But she also needed to acknowledge how consequential that weekend was, how his attention, in some strange way, encouraged her to gather her strength and finally move on from her train wreck marriage. Just being with him gave her the confidence to gather her wits and courage to start again.

'Thank you for being there for me that weekend,' she said, unable to look at him.

'Rescuing you from that prick was the least I could do,' he muttered, frowning.

'You rescued me from more than just being in his presence,' she explained. 'You told me I was strong and capable and that I deserved more. In the months following that night, when things got really tough, and they got really tough, I held on to your words, and often reminded myself that somewhere in the world, some hot guy thought I was courageous. And strong and worthy of more.'

Judah stroked her hair, her bare back. 'You forgot sexy and gorgeous.'

Was it the heat from the sun causing her cheeks to bloom, or was it the way he looked at her, like she was a much-anticipated birthday gift he couldn't wait to unwrap? His eyes dropped to her mouth, and Calla swallowed, longing to straddle his thighs and lay her mouth on his. She wanted him, wanted more of him, wanted more...

But wanting more was dangerous, and she didn't know how to want without considering the consequences. She was risking her independence, all the work she'd done on herself, for herself, to get to this place in her life where she felt capable and strong. She couldn't allow a man to slide back into her life and take over. And Judah, despite being younger than her, was a take-charge type of guy. He wouldn't sit on the sidelines, waiting for her permission to walk into her life, happy to leave it when she felt the need for solitude. She could never risk allowing anybody to mess with her psyche and soul. She couldn't even suggest a one-night, or couple-of-nights stand with Judah, because she knew that the closer she got to him, the more she'd want. Her imagination would start working overtime, and she'd start to want more than she could have.

Lovely things. Impossible things.

'It's not a good idea, Judah.'

He didn't pretend to misunderstand her. 'Probably not. But I can't stop myself from wanting you.'

Having such a big, masculine, alpha man look at her with desire-fuelled fire in his eyes made her feel powerful and feminine, like she was channelling every goddess throughout the centuries. She knew it was a siren's call, a way to madness, but she couldn't help leaning sideways, her mouth finding his.

Judah cradled her face in his hand, his thumb stroking her cheek bone. 'Stop overthinking this, sweetheart.' His deep voice was low, coaxing, and a little wistful. 'Let's pretend, just for a couple of hours, the rest of the day, that we are who we were back then. I'm just a bartender, and you're a woman who walked out of the bar with me.'

Calla's heart lurched. His soft request was ridiculous. And dangerous, but so, so intoxicating. She should say no. She should scoot away, thank him for the trip to the beach and ask him to take her home so she could get back to work. Once there, she would sit at a desk and wait for inspiration to strike.

But she didn't move.

She looked into his eyes and felt her resolve dissolving. He dropped his hand and lifted an eyebrow, but she didn't feel pressured or manipulated. He was just asking, and Calla knew that if she found the strength to say no, he wouldn't sulk or curse, he'd simply respect her decision. Unlike Jack, he was a grown-up.

As the seconds ticked past, she found it more and more difficult to distance herself from him. She'd wanted him back then; she wanted him now. Wasn't she allowed this? One little (or big) indulgence? She was, generally, a good person, someone who worked hard, played fair and did her best to be nice. Was responsible. Surely she was allowed a moment where she got to take and feast? She wasn't asking for forever or for a promise of something more. She just wanted him. For a little while. And when the time came, she'd be able to let him go. She had to.

Calla closed her eyes. 'Okay,' she whispered. 'Let's pretend.'

CHAPTER SEVEN

JUDAH ABRUPTLY BRAKED, exited the Jeep and ran around to the passenger door, ripping it open. He'd kept hold of Calla's hand the entire journey home, terrified her rational, careful brain would talk her out of letting him take her to bed.

He wrenched her door open and unclicked her safety belt, her perfume going straight to his head. Pulling back, her mouth inches from his, he watched her eyelids lower as she looked at his lips, her clenched fist resting on her thigh. She wanted him…

Just to make sure, he covered her mouth with his and slid his tongue between her teeth, lightly growling as he took her mouth, spicy and fresh, on fire for him. Knowing he needed nothing but her, only her, he slid his one hand under her thighs, the other around her back and easily lifted her out of the car, hurrying to the front door of his house. Holding her easily, he walked her inside and up the stone staircase to the master suite, a place he'd longed to take her since first seeing her.

Judah laid Calla on his big bed, pulling back to take her in. She still wore her board shorts and her bikini, but she'd lost a flip-flop somewhere between the car and his bedroom. Her hair tumbled over her pink-from-the-sun shoulders, and her eyes were wide and full of heat and want. A deep, dark green that reminded him of mystical and ancient forests, a place where druids worshipped and spirits roamed. She lifted her hand and traced the ball of his shoulder with her index finger, and she followed its path down his pec and over his nipple. He closed his eyes.

Her touch felt like home.

'Your body is perfection, Judah,' she said on a breathy sigh that sent a bolt of heat and electricity straight down his spine. Oh, his body wasn't perfect, he knew that—he had scars on his collarbone, chin, a nasty one on his shoulder from surgery, more scars on his thigh from a car accident. But he wasn't going to argue with her…

'So strong, so masculine, so powerful.' Calla sat up and linked her hands around his neck. 'Kiss me, Judah. I like it when you kiss me.'

His liking started with her breathing, and it just got worse from there. 'Are you sure this is what you want, Cal?' he asked. It was so hard to check in when all he wanted to do was take and take and take. But he needed her fully on board, and yes, his ego wanted to hear that she wanted him as much as he wanted her.

'Mm,' she said, lifting her left shoulder. He couldn't resist her soft, smooth skin, so he dropped an open-mouthed kiss on her collarbone.

Not good enough. He needed more. 'Is that a yes, Calla?'

She planted a series of small kisses on his jaw. 'It is,' she said, and he noted the lack of hesitation in her voice. Judah pushed her back and lowered himself to her, keeping his weight off her by digging his elbow into the mattress. He stroked her hair away from her face and smiled.

'You are so goddamn beautiful, Calla,' he murmured, before placing his mouth on hers. He simply rested his mouth on hers, happy to let their anticipation build, knowing that gratification would be so much hotter and sweeter later.

Calla, more impatient than he, pushed her tongue to trace the seam of his lips, to tempt him with tiny nibbles that tested his resolve. The urge to take nearly overwhelmed him, but he knew he had to go slow, or else this would be all over far too soon. Calla needed, deserved more. They both did. They were both in the ring, punching it out with circumstances and life. Calla was fighting the memories of her past, trying to plant her feet, and he was trying to reclaim himself, the pieces he'd lost over the past few years. Fighting to figure out who he was while trying not to be drowned out by the noise of the world shouting who he should be.

But for tonight, for however long he had to love her—because God, being with her was *everything*—he'd make sure they forgot the mental wars they were waging. They would, as the many lifestyle coaches and yoga instructors he employed instructed, be present.

'Judah.'

The way she said his name, holding a little bit of wonder, a lot of need, skittered through him, and he pulled back to take in her lovely face. So pretty, the only woman who'd ever managed to slide beneath the surface, the one he couldn't hide from. Or not completely. Man, he wanted her.

Sliding his arm under her waist, he pulled her up and into him and covered her mouth, unable to go slow, needing to take, and give. His tongue twisted around hers; Calla released a moan and dug her fingernails into his shoulders. Sweet pain. Her hand drifted down his back, and she pushed her hand under the band of his swim shorts, frustrated when the barrier of the fabric impeded her progress. Oh, he'd shed his clothes, but not yet.

Today, with her, the journey was as important as the destination.

Lowering her back down to the bed, he moved his mouth along her jaw, down her neck and across her collarbone, pulling aside the straps of her bikini top as he went. He was about to undo the clasp when Calla half sat and did it for him, pulling the top away and flinging it to the ground. Judah immediately rewarded her by locking onto a perfect, already hard nipple, lathing it with his tongue. His fingers covered her other breast, testing its weight, his thumb teasing her nipple. How was it that her skin tasted so sweet?

He'd never been this hard, this desperate to be inside a woman, longing to experience her wet warmth. With hands that were less assured than normal, his breathing more ragged, he pushed her shorts down her hips, taking her bikini bottoms with them. This…Calla…naked. Lying on his bed as the dappled sunlight hit the bed, just as he'd dreamed. His.

For now.

Judah rolled off the bed and stood up to shuck his shorts, his eyes on her face. He liked that she lay there and looked her fill. He did the same. Long legs, round hips, a mole on her right hip. His eyes locked on hers, and he fell into all that green, another walk through that ancient and mysterious forest. What was she thinking? He was desperate to know.

Calla sat up and encircled him. 'You're so beautiful,' she told him, sounding serious. 'I look at you and all the moisture from my mouth disappears.'

Judah wasn't used to compliments from his lovers; they generally expected to hear them, and rarely handed them out. A little dazed by the emotions skipping through her eyes—so much lust, a little affection—he placed his hand on top of hers to keep her from stroking him. 'If you keep doing that, I'm going to come.' He wasn't lying; when it came to her, he had minimal self-control.

He placed one hand next to her head and slid his other hand down, over her stomach, between her legs, finding her sensitive spot without hesitation. She arched off the bed, closed her eyes and released a long, huffy breath. The fantastic combination of sea, her perfume and sex wafted over them, and Judah groaned. He was a grown man, experienced, but he didn't know how much longer he could keep himself from plunging into her, from losing himself in her. He was on a knife's edge here.

But he needed to make Calla come first. Two for her, one for him…that was the deal, a silent promise to every woman he made love to. If they were gracious enough to give him their bodies, it was the least he could do.

Judah rested his thumb on her. Her breathing was as ragged as his. Calla's mouth dropped open, and he was about to kiss her when she rested her fingers on his jaw, her face and body flushed with pleasure.

'I'm so close.'

He was aware and loved that she was so responsive. 'No more,' she said, pushing his hand away. What the hell? Why was she stopping now? Judah hesitated, unsure why she was slamming on the brakes. Calla rubbed her thumb over his bottom lip.

'It might sound corny, very uncool, but I want us to come together, like we did back then.'

He loved her honesty and didn't care about being corny or being cool. And, well, he wanted that too, obviously. But that would break his rule of two to one. When he hesitated, Calla narrowed her eyes. 'I'm not sure what you're thinking right now, but if you don't get a condom on in the next two seconds, I might scream. And not in pleasure.'

Right. God. What was he waiting for? This was Calla, not a casual hookup. There were no rules when it came to her, he was stumbling around in the dark. Shocked into action, Judah managed to open the bedside drawer without looking and found a strip of condoms. He pulled it out, ripped one off and tossed the rest on the bed, or maybe they landed on the floor. He didn't care; he'd look for them later. Calla, impatient, took the packet, removed the condom and slid over him. He loved her hand stroking him. She felt…right. Hot and exciting but comfortable too. Safe.

Weird to be feeling that right now. He was about to cover her, to finally, finally, slide home, when Calla pushed him onto his back and threw her leg over his hips. She closed her eyes as she rocked against him. All doubts about whether she was ready evaporated as he took in her expression, a combination of warrior want and feminine power. She lowered herself onto him, inch by fabulous inch, biting her lip every time a wave of pleasure rippled through her. He could feel her every reaction, and pleasure spiked through him. She rocked, he lifted, the room faded away, and all that was left was Calla.

Knowing he couldn't wait a second longer, Judah rolled her over and in one fluid move, made her his. He checked once, quickly, to see if she was okay and still with him—her glazed eyes and open mouth told him she was—and then started to move, Calla following where he led. Hot and strong, hips lifting in sync, they reached for and gathered every last molecule of concentrated pleasure. Energy rocketed down his spine, but he wouldn't go there without her.

'Calla, now,' he commanded. He needed her in this moment with him.

'Now?' she asked, breathless.

He dropped an F-bomb and clenched her hip, digging his fingertips into her soft skin. He was holding on by a thread now.

'Okay,' Calla said on a breathy laugh, and he felt her ripple, heard her pleasure-filled sob. Thank God. He could let go, so he did, diving in again, chasing that special high he hadn't felt since her. That added extra, something indefinable, and only experienced with Calla. The room filled with colour, an aura pulsed behind his eyes, and then he shattered, coming hard. All that was left was a vortex of sensation, and Calla standing in the middle of it.

Somewhere, from a place far away, he felt Calla's hips lift, her back arch, her small whimper, her body rippling as pleasure rolled through her a second time. He rested his forehead on her collarbone and smiled.

Two for one. Yeah. The way it should be.

This was straight out of a romance movie.

Calla, her back to Judah's chest, her head on his bicep, his leg over hers, looked out of one of the two glass doors that formed the walls of the master suite. Across the bay, Buck Island looked greener today, the sea a more intense shade of blue. A speedboat flew across the slightly choppy waters, and a yacht with sails unfurled headed out to sea. Where were they going? To the Bahamas or Jamaica?

Talking of…where was she going? Where was this going? She and Judah spent the rest of yesterday and most of last night making love—they hadn't been able to stop, well, feasting was an accurate description—and they'd only fallen asleep a few hours ago. But it was morning now; she'd woken at her normal time, and the reality of her situation strolled back in and parked its arse down. And while spending concentrated, naked time with Judah had been lovely, nothing had, fundamentally, changed.

She still needed to protect her business, and herself, from Jack's never-ending insinuations and manipulations, and to establish herself so firmly that nothing he or his family said or did could undermine her or her business. That meant landing a high-profile client, a client that screamed 'she'd arrived' and 'don't mess with her'. Judah was that client, her one shot. And she'd jeopardised everything by sleeping with him.

Oh, he'd promised their personal history wouldn't affect any business decisions—and she wanted to believe him. But reality was that, by giving in to temptation, she'd added a layer of unneeded complication. She'd put everything at risk to be with him.

How stupid was that? She'd done that with Jack, and look where that got her. She'd lost her share of the business, all her savings, and had her heart stomped on. And he was still trying to hurt her in any way he could. But here she was, in Judah's arms, practically begging life to test her again.

When would she learn?

She needed to get out of his bed, leave his room and reset their relationship. Get back on track. Now. Immediately. And it would be so much better if she could do that without hashing it out, without any explanations. She'd leave, and when she saw him again, she'd treat him like her client and be super professional and polite. With luck, he'd get her '*this was a mistake*' message.

Calla, hearing his deep breathing, pulled her leg from under his and lifted her head off his arm. She wrapped her hand around his wrist and lifted his arm—man, it was heavy—off her chest, rolling away from him. Landing on her feet, she stared down at him, holding her breath. When he didn't move, she released a long stream of pent-up air.

So far, so good.

Spotting one of his shirts lying over the back of an easy chair, she pulled it over her head, the soft hem hitting her thighs. Where were her clothes? Her bikini top lay at the end of the bed, and her bottoms and shorts were on the floor. One flip-flop, where was the other?

She couldn't find it and decided to look for it later. Her main objective was to leave his room without him realising she was gone, without having to talk to him. Because if he looked at her with those marvellous blue eyes, if she saw his sexy half-smile, she might be tempted to climb back into that ridiculously big bed and play hooky for the day, the week.

She had work to do, a company to run, a design to submit, a future to secure. No man, not even Judah Reyes, would knock her off course again.

Calla tiptoed to the door, the light wood floor silky beneath her bare feet. Grabbing the handle to slide open the door, she turned back to look at him and gasped. Judah rested on his elbows, his hair mussed and his eyes narrowed. 'Were you seriously going to sneak out?' he demanded.

Calla wrinkled her nose; she was so busted. She rubbed her foot on the back of her calf. 'I—um—I thought I'd let you sleep.'

He rubbed his hand over his stubbled jaw, unimpressed by her obvious lie. 'No, you're leaving because you're trying to put distance between us, distance between the person you were last night and the person you're trying to be.'

What did that even mean?

Judah left the bed and walked over to her, supremely comfortable in his nakedness. And why shouldn't he be? He was gorgeous. He stood in front of her and placed his forearm on the door above her head, caging her in. It took everything within Calla not to lay her cheek on his chest, plaster her body against his. No, she had to be strong. This was another one-night thing, just two ships passing and all that. They were ships that should never have collided...and what was with the references to ships? *Honestly.*

'Why are you running, Calla?'

She wasn't, precisely, running. Maybe walking fast? But she couldn't tell Judah she was terrified of how he made her feel. He sparked her imagination of what could be, of the future she'd dreamed of when she was young and naive. She could barely admit it to herself, never mind to him, that he made her feel loved, cherished and protected.

But protecting her wasn't his job; it wasn't anyone's job. She was her own protector, her biggest advocate, her only cheerleader. Asking anyone else to do that for her, to give them that much responsibility, was asking to be disappointed.

She'd write her own story. Create her own life. Live it alone.

She forced herself to meet his eyes. They could both benefit from some honesty. 'I slept with my client, Judah. What does that make me?' she asked, her voice breaking a little.

'The hell you slept with a client, Calla!' Okay, so he wasn't going to let that stand. 'You slept with *me*. The man you met ten months back, the one who walked you out of the Reyes Luxe bar. You did not sleep with the owner of Reyes Luxe. That's what we agreed yesterday.'

She threw up her hands, frustrated. 'We just used that as an excuse to sleep together! We both know we can't separate the two!' Calla cried. 'It doesn't work that way.'

His eyes hardened, and she caught a glimpse of the determined businessman who made tough decisions involving millions of dollars and affecting thousands. 'It does if I say it does,' he said, not yielding an inch. 'Your work has nothing to do with what we did last night. Our personal interactions are between you and me. Do *not* confuse the two.'

How could she not when so much was on the line? 'That's easy to say when you're not the one who's risking everything, Judah, when it's not your butt dangling over the fire. You hold the power—I have none.'

His jaw tightened, and she suspected he was grinding his teeth. 'It's not about power, Calla.'

She released a sharp sigh. 'Of course it is, Judah. Everything is about control and power. You have it, I do not. You can change my life, businesswise, but nothing I do or say will affect you. You hold all the cards. And that's why this,' she waggled her index finger between them, 'will never happen again.'

The problem was that he just had to look at her and her knees weakened, and her body throbbed from wanting him. Tough. She'd just have to suck it up and remember the big picture. He held her future in his hands, and she'd jeopardised their professional relationship by taking a stroll through the past and hooking up with him again. Stupid. This was why her body and heart should never be allowed to make decisions.

'I'm going to shower and get to work. I already lost too much time yesterday.' Calla ducked under his arm and, when she was out of his reach, turned back to look at him. 'And I'd appreciate it if we could forget this happened. I'd like us to go back to being client and decorator.'

Keeping his hands on the wall, he turned his head to look at her, his blue eyes lasering through her. 'Let me think about that...mm.' He waited a beat before speaking again. 'No, we're not going to do that.'

Right. She was on her own, fighting their attraction. That was okay; she'd fought bigger battles than facing down a sexy man who wanted her. She could do this.

Maybe.

She hoped.

One step forward. Six back.

Judah pulled on a pair of shorts, sat on the edge of his bed, his forearms on his knees as he listened to Calla's retreating footsteps. He hadn't expected her to stay all day, but he'd at least hoped for the morning. He'd had plans for her; he'd wanted to see her sleep-soaked eyes turn limp and liquid with desire, wanted to wake her up with slow morning sex. He'd wanted to drink coffee with her on his bedroom balcony, as they watched the activity in the bay. Wanted to take her back to bed for a mid-morning nap.

But she was gone—already slipping back behind her walls.

He exhaled hard and scrubbed a hand over his jaw. He got it. He did. Still, it didn't stop the sting.

With Calla, he felt like himself. Just Judah. With her, he felt like he did last year, like he was wholly, completely himself, not a satellite of his father or Reyes Luxe's highest-paid minion. Back then, she hadn't known who he was, and he'd loved the anonymity. He had been seen for who he really was, not what he owned, ran or represented. She'd made him feel that way again last night, and something inside him had readjusted. Like his heart could finally beat without being squeezed tight.

Losing his father had thrown everything into chaos. David Reyes had been a good father in many ways, but he'd also been a lot to deal with. Bigger than life, relentless in his vision and driven to make Reyes Luxe the number one wellness brand in the world.

And then his father died. And the world expected him to take the reins of the company, ready or not. After ten long, exhausting months, he was remembering what it felt like to have loose lungs, shoulder blades that weren't tight with tension, how it felt to move through the day without a dull, just-there headache. To think. To dream about the future, not to just worry about it. Ideas were starting to bubble, and thoughts about where he could take Reyes Luxe and how he could put his own mark on the company, flitted in and out of his mind. They were still nebulous, unformed, but it was his vision, not his father's. Something quieter, a brand that was less in your face. Something more real and accessible.

Calla, as he somehow sensed she would, reminded him of who he was and the man he wanted to be. Reconnecting with Calla had shifted something in him. He hadn't realised quite how numb he'd been until she walked back into his life…until her laughter warmed the rooms, her voice soothed his soul and her smile kick-started his heart. Now that they'd slept together—and he'd seen her briefly drop her guard—he couldn't pretend nothing had changed.

She saw beyond the brand and his CEO image, had told him to trust his gut, and to stop chasing his father's version of success. But she wasn't living her life that way. She was still letting fear run the show, keeping it all strictly professional like that might protect her from feeling too much.

But he also understood her hesitation. The power imbalance between them was real. And like any other professional with a sense of pride, she didn't want his charity and wanted to keep her talent separate from their chemistry. Just like he wanted to keep himself separate from Reyes Luxe, from his dad. He respected her stance.

But did she understand how good her designs were? She had a great eye for colour, and a clean but expressive style with an audacious edge. Just like he'd wanted to earn his place at Reyes Luxe, Calla wanted the commission to redesign Sol House because she nailed the brief, not because they nearly set the sheets alight.

Still...*shit*. He liked her. In a deeper, harder way than he had back then. He liked her mind. Her stubbornness. Those flashes of vulnerability that seeped out when she wasn't careful. Her courage and her strength to keep going. Sure, there was a part of him that ached to protect her—with his money and connections, he could make life easy for her. But she'd hate that. And it would make her hate him. Calla didn't need a white knight, she needed a man who believed in her.

Could he be that person?

Judah pushed both hands into his hair, tugged. He'd only recently reconnected with her, and was trying to figure out his way forward. Right now, he couldn't offer her much beyond great sex. He was in a state of flux himself, his own road unclear. But, despite saying that, he knew he wasn't just looking for another one-night stand with Calla. And he couldn't pretend their chemistry and attraction would go away just because she wanted it to.

But for now, maybe they did need to hit Pause. That was the sensible, adult choice. Just until the ground under his feet stopped shifting, until a clear path opened up ahead. He knew what he should do…but after a night like that, how was he supposed to just walk away?

CHAPTER EIGHT

JUDAH HELD CALLA'S tablet and squinted at it. The colour palette was shades of white, with splashes of island colour, reds and tangerines, hot pinks, all the colours of a Caribbean sunset. It radiated easy comfort—plush, sink-right-in sofas, a coffee table sturdy enough for sun-kissed feet, and lush, vibrant indoor plants. It was a space he could live in, the kind that made his shoulders drop, his tension ease. And yet, somehow, it still felt elegant. Stylish enough to impress, but warm enough to unwind in. God, she was talented. He tapped the screen with his index finger before angling the screen so Calla could look at it.

'I like this,' he said.

Calla, standing opposite him at the head of the outdoor dining table, pulled her bottom lip between her teeth. He ached to soothe the slight pain with his lips. It had been two days since they'd made love. Calla had holed up in the guest cottage, seldom leaving. He saw the light on in the cottage late at night, and he knew she was burning the midnight oil. There were also dark stripes under her eyes, and she looked a little pale. He wanted to take her to bed but knew that as soon as he got her horizontal, she'd probably slide off into sleep. He was more than happy to hold her while she slept and was prepared to be any type of pillow she required.

He jammed his hands into the pockets of his shorts. 'Stop biting your lip, Calla. There's no reason to be nervous.'

Her lip popped out, and she folded her arms, rocking on her heels. 'I really want you to like them,' she said, and Judah picked up the anxiety in her voice. 'I mean, I want all my clients to like my designs…'

He sighed. Why was she avoiding him, wasting the little time they had? It was stupid, and asinine. They were adults, they liked each other and wanted to sleep with each other. Why did this have to be more complicated than that? Why was she throwing work into the mix, and why was he worried about what came next? Why couldn't they live in the present?

'This is close,' he told her, tapping the screen. 'Maybe fewer white couches?'

Calla nodded. 'I can do that. It was my favourite too, but I thought the pinks and reds would put you off.'

Not even close. He half sat on the table. 'This

is going to be a once-in-ten-years overhaul, so I want it to be able to withstand people coming in and out, and them using the furniture. And white isn't practical for a beach house.'

'You want it kid and dog proof,' she murmured. She kept her eyes on the mood board, but her cheeks flushed with a shade of pink similar to the swoosh on the mood board. Was that her way of asking whether he wanted either, or both, in the future? A way for her to take a few steps back to him?

'I want both, at some point,' he told her. He gestured to the great room and then pointed to the pool. 'I want them to play Lego on the floor, swim in the pool.'

'The kids or the dogs?'

He smiled. 'Either. Both,' he replied, then grinned. 'A Lego-playing dog would be cool.' He folded his arms, enjoying her laughter. 'Do you want kids?' he asked.

'I did...' She hesitated. 'I do. But I've been consumed with my business for so long that I haven't spent much time thinking about it. Also, I know how hard it is to be a single parent, so I don't want to do it alone. But I'm nudging forty, so I'm running out of time.'

No, she wasn't, that was nonsense. Plenty of women had children in their early to mid-forties these days. The image of Calla, her tummy round with her child, grinning at him, flashed behind his eyes, and it was so strong and so perfect that his knees jellified.

Judah rubbed his hand over his face, around the back of his neck, feeling hot and clammy. He'd spent the morning paddleboarding, maybe he'd spent too much time in the hot sun and was suffering from a little heat stroke. Kids weren't on his radar, and since he was only in his early thirties, he had lots of time. After he sorted out Reyes Luxe, reengineered it and reshaped it, he could think about settling down, being a dad.

But that would only be in about ten years or so…

And while he had time, ten years was pushing the boundaries of Calla's fertility. *God... enough, Judah. You're jumping too far ahead. You've only slept with the woman a few times. Maybe you should sort your professional life out first before planning your personal.*

Judah's phone vibrated, bouncing slightly against the wooden surface of the table, and he looked down at the screen. Grateful for the distraction, he answered his assistant's call. 'Yeah, what is it?'

He listened to Brent's explanation for his call, his blood icing. After five minutes, he spoke. 'Let me get this straight…. The board isn't prepared to wait for my decision about acquiring ForgeRitual?'

'They are demanding a decision within a week.'

'I am the bloody CEO and the major shareholder of this company,' Judah muttered, his words gritty. 'I'm not sold on their brand, I think it flirts with toxic masculinity.'

'They disagree and they think this is too good an opportunity to lose.'

Judah swore, and his eyes connected with Calla's. She cradled her tablet to her chest, her expression concerned. 'Are you okay?' she mouthed.

Obviously all his irritation was reflected on his face. It seemed he lost his ability to look unaffected around her. He shook his head, and she winced.

'Also...'

Oh, crap, he instantly recognised the anxiety in that one word. What else had gone wrong? 'Did you see the email from Harmony Green?' Brent asked.

Reyes Luxe's head of research was emailing him? Harmony, a close friend of his dad's and one of David's first hires, called him directly when she had an issue. 'What does the email say?'

'Look for it. I'll wait while you read it.'

What was going on, and why did Brent sound so deflated? Judah read the email. He turned hot, then cold, and goose bumps covered his skin. What fresh hell was this?

Calla walked over to him, carrying two beers in one hand and Judah's sunglasses in the other. After abruptly disconnecting his phone call, he'd walked up to the railing, his face white and his lips bloodless.

Had someone died? Did the bottom fall out of Reyes Luxe's stock price? Was his enormous workforce going on strike? She tapped his arm with one of the bottles, and when he looked at her, she pushed the beer into one hand and his sunglasses into the other.

'Thanks,' he said, his voice hollow. Judah placed the bottle on the railing, his fingers white against the bright green bottle. Yeah, something had rocked him. But what? Judah was normally so unreadable, so calm and collected—okay, except when he made love to her—so it was a surprise to see him with messy hair and turbulent eyes, his expression frustrated and a little uncertain.

She needed to comfort him, but didn't know how. Scooting closer to him, she pushed her shoulder into his arm and tipped her head to rest her temple on his shoulder. 'What happened?'

Judah didn't answer her, choosing instead to look at his phone. He swiped his thumb over the screen and shoved it at her. Calla took it and saw that it was an email from someone called Harmony Green. Judging by the domain name at the end of her address, she worked at Reyes Luxe.

Calla skimmed through the email...

We've had several conversations about the future of Reyes Luxe and your intention to honour your father's legacy...

However, I've recently learned that Reyes Luxe is seriously considering a partnership with Forge-Ritual. I want to be clear: I believe this would be a serious misstep for the brand....

Over the past few years, I often challenged David's choices as the company veered toward scale over substance, and I came close to resigning. I ultimately chose to stay because I believed in your leadership and your potential to steer the company with authenticity.

But your willingness to even entertain this partnership has shaken that belief...

Regrettably, I no longer feel I can continue with the company under this direction.

Wow. Calla tapped the side button to turn the screen black. She placed the phone on the dining table and walked back to where Judah stood, his jaw clenched, still looking out to sea. He'd yet to put on his sunglasses or take a sip from his beer.

She placed her back to the railing and the sea. 'I remember you mentioning ForgeRitual, Judah. It's a men's wellness brand, right?' They promoted men's-only gyms and spas, vitamins to boost testosterone and leaned into 'reclaim your masculinity' branding.

'The business plan says acquiring it is a no-brainer. We'll recoup the investment in a year and will double profits in eighteen months. My board members keep telling me it will honour my father's legacy as a man's man who built his body and his business.'

'Is that what you think?' Calla gently asked.

'They keep reminding me of our investors, that we need to keep expanding into new markets, of my father's legacy.'

'But this won't be his legacy, Judah, it will be *yours*,' Calla pointed out. 'It'll carry your name, and it will be your signature on the deal.' The whole concept sounded dreadful, and she instinctively hated it. But this wasn't about her—it was about Judah and how he saw his company and his role within it. Would he chase profits? Did he care about what people thought about him, what he'd leave behind as a legacy? How much did he owe his father, and how far would he go to honour the man he loved and adored?

'My father trusted the board, trusted his advisers,' Judah stated.

'But?'

He finally looked at her.

Judah's grip on the beer bottle finally loosened. He slid his sunglasses over his eyes and lifted the bottle to his lips. After a few swallows and a long moment of silence, he spoke again. 'The men on the board, my father's friends, chase profits. That's what they do.' He nodded at his phone. 'This would be a very profitable venture.'

'But you're not convinced.'

'How do you know that?' Judah asked, half turning and leaning his hip into the stone wall. The sun turned the stubble on his jaw and the hair on his arms golden. In his polo shirt and chino shorts, he looked every inch the rich millionaire he was. But there was tension in his thin lips, and in the tight muscles in his neck and shoulders.

'Well, you mentioned as much before. You've delayed making the decision because you aren't certain, not because you are. I think your first impression was right, Judah.'

'And what was my first impression?' Judah asked, knocking his bottle against his thigh.

'That you absolutely bloody hate it.' Calla was surprised by how certain she sounded, how convincing. Judah didn't believe in toxic masculinity. Of course he would hate the idea.

Instead of answering her, Judah slid his arm around her waist and pulled her into him. What else could she do but clutch his shirt and rest her cheek on his hard chest? How could she stay professional when he needed comfort and connection? She felt his lips in her hair, the light kiss he placed on her temple. His hand on her lower back pulled her closer, and her stomach hit the hard ridge of his erection…he *wanted* her. No, he wanted her a *lot*.

She stiffened, and Judah released a half-laugh, half snort. 'I can't hold you and not want you, Calla. That's asking too much of me.'

Calla leaned back to look up into his gorgeous face, frowning when he simply held her, not speaking. Not pushing.

That was all? Why wasn't he demanding more, kissing her, coaxing her back into his bed? And why did she feel so disappointed? If keeping things professional between them meant so much to her, if it was so important, why did she keep digging into his thoughts and life, and listen when he spoke about his problems? Why couldn't she keep any decent sort of emotional distance between them?

And why did she want to kiss him again, make love to him, here in the sunlight in the middle of a scorching July day?

'Your eyes...' Judah murmured, his hand coming up to caress the skin under her right eye. 'They're warm and full of heat. They tell me you want me, Calla.'

She should protest, deny his words, but her tongue refused to cooperate. It couldn't form the words.

'Being apart from you, not being able to touch you, has been hell, Cal. Tell me you want me to take you to bed, Calla.'

She should pull away, insist that she needed to go back to work, to keep their relationship on a business footing. But she couldn't. The only thing she wanted was to get naked with him, right here and now.

Don't do it, Calla, it'll be another mistake.

But it was a mistake she could live with, would have to live with, because she wanted this memory. One day, when she was old and wrinkled, and sex was a distant memory, she wanted to recall making love with Judah in the sunlight, the Caribbean glinting blue beneath them, sunlight dancing on Judah's skin as he pleasured her.

She wouldn't deny future Calla this memory…

Standing on her tiptoes, Calla slid her hands under Judah's shirt, finding hot skin covering hard muscles. After brushing her mouth across his, she tugged his shirt up and over his head, exposing his tanned chest and abs, his big arms. His shirt dropped to the floor. His shorts rode low on his hips. So hot. So sexy.

And for now, the next hour, day, week or two, he was hers.

'Make love to me, Judah,' she murmured. His eyes darkened with heat and need, and when he dipped his knees to scoop her up to carry her inside, she stepped back and put a hand on his shoulder. When his eyes slammed into hers, she shook his head and smiled at his cocked eyebrow.

She nodded to a double bed lounger half in and half out of the sun. 'We're completely alone. Why not here? And why not now?'

He pushed back a strand of her hair that had escaped her functional ponytail. Needing to feel it wrapped around his hand, he tugged the band from her hair, and her wavy hair spilt down her back and over her shoulders. 'I need to go inside to get a condom, but I'm scared to leave you alone in case you change your mind.'

Sweet of him, but she had a solution for that problem. Her hand skated across his chest, over the ball of his shoulder, down his big arm. 'I'm on the pill and haven't had sex since you last year.'

'I had a physical a few weeks ago. I'm clean.'

'If you want, we can—'

'I want.'

Calla squealed when Judah banded his arm around her waist, lifted her off her feet and walked her over to the lounger, where he placed her on her feet. He gently turned her around, found the zipper to her sundress and slid it down her back, his lips following the path of the zip as he lowered it, his lips hot against her skin.

He kicked her dress away and turned her to face him, and traced a finger over the edge of the cup of her sky blue bra. Thankfully, her panties matched today; they didn't always. 'I missed you. Sometimes I look at you and everything disappears.'

She knew what he meant, sometimes it felt like they were the only two inhabitants on earth, that the world and everything in it had faded into insignificance. It was so terrifying being so in tune with someone.

Because she wanted to lighten the atmosphere, to bring them back to the moment, and the pleasure they were about to enjoy, Calla reached behind her back and unsnapped her bra. The cups fell away and Judah gently pulled it from her body and let it land on her sundress.

'Yeah, this is going to be one of those memories I keep forever,' he murmured, his hand covering her breast, his thumb rubbing her nipple into a hard, tight peak.

They were in sync again. What was she going to do about it?

Dressed in Judah's shirt, Calla rolled onto her side on the two-person lounger and placed her hands under her cheek. Judah had pulled on his shorts and lay on his back next to her, one hand under his head, his other hand resting on her hip.

She should feel guilty about sleeping with him again, but she didn't. She felt like a woman, at ease in her skin, appreciated and adored by her lover, satiated and relaxed. She knew she should be working, but she'd worked so hard for so long. Surely she was allowed to take an afternoon off now and again?

'Cal?'

'Mm?' She was feeling a little dozy, and could, without any effort at all, drift off to sleep.

'Tell me what happened with your ex.' Calla frowned. That was an out of the blue question. She was now fully awake and deeply uncomfortable. She hated talking about Jack. He was a reminder of how she'd been, how naive, how she thought love would solve all her life problems.

'Why do you want to know?' she asked, sitting up and crossing her legs. Judah didn't move, he just looked at her with eyes that could laser through her.

'I want to know you,' he said. 'You are the person you are today because of the things that happened to you. I've picked up bits and pieces, things you told me back then and now, but I want to hear the full story, all at once.' He frowned. 'And I want to know whether I should've hit him when he walked into the bar.'

His statement raised a small smile, but it quickly fell away. 'It's not a pretty story, Judah.'

'Marriages that fall apart usually aren't,' he agreed. 'That doesn't mean the stories aren't worth telling.'

Calla looked down at her hands twisting together in her lap. She needed to be honest with him, because it was the only way to make him understand why this could never go anywhere, why she would never allow herself to be in a relationship again.

But telling him meant more than just recounting her history. It meant showing him how weak she'd been. How easily Jack had broken her down, that it had taken so very long for her to realise he didn't love her but just wanted control over her. She had clawed her way to find her self-respect, but to lay it bare for someone like Judah? Someone smart, self-possessed and capable? She didn't want him to see her like that.

She had her pride. And pride was the only thing that had kept her going. And her pride still didn't want to tell him the truth. That Jack eviscerated her, and that the idea of depending on and trusting someone still made her flinch. If she told him, he'd understand the depth of her resolve, but he'd also see that she'd been naive. And so damn weak.

She didn't want him looking at her and seeing those cracked and battered parts of her.

He squeezed her knee. 'I think you desperately need to tell someone, Calla, and it might as well be me.'

Calla wrinkled her nose. Nobody, apart from her divorce lawyer, knew of the hoops Jack made her jump through, the levels of hell he made her walk through. Her lawyer even went so far as to urge her to have therapy, but she'd chosen to shove away the pain and disillusionment and bury herself in her work.

But Judah was here and willing to listen and wouldn't, she didn't think, judge her too harshly. 'While I was working to midnight every night, designing homes that got us noticed, that even won some awards and accolades, Jack was spending his time cheating on me and embezzling funds from our joint business account.'

'Bastard,' Judah muttered.

'Worse, he used my designs—my ideas—to secure contracts under a new design company he quietly established. Over a few years, he moved our jointly owned assets into shell companies by duping me about what I was signing, sometimes even by cleverly forging my signature.'

Judah sat up and ran a hand over her hair, his touch immediately dropping her rising anger levels. 'Then he locked me out of business decisions. When I couldn't ignore it any longer, I demanded a divorce. During those negotiations, his legal team painted me as being—how did they put it?—emotionally unstable and professionally incompetent.'

'He's the human version of a haemorrhoid,' Judah said, his words a low growl.

'The fallout was devastating. I lost my stake in the company, the one I grew and nurtured. I lost my talented staff, who I'd trained and mentored. My client list.'

She swallowed and swallowed again. 'Worst of all, I lost my reputation and my credibility. I wasn't just heartbroken—he humiliated me. I'm furious that he did that to me, that I *allowed* him to do that to me.'

It wasn't until Judah gently wiped away a tear

that she realised she was crying. She used the balls of her hands to remove the moisture from her cheeks and chin. 'I hate crying,' she muttered.

'I think you haven't cried enough, sweetheart,' Judah told her, banding his arm around her waist to pull her onto his lap. Clasping her head to his bare chest, he wrapped his arms around her and kissed the top of her head. 'He doesn't deserve your tears, but you're allowed to cry. You must've felt so alone, so hurt, like you were caught under a tsunami of betrayal.'

He got her, like no one had before. Calla felt a sob build, tried to push it down, and another rolled over it, stronger and wilder, and up her throat. Calla tried to pull away from Judah—quiet tears were one thing for him to witness, her losing it was another—but he just tightened his arms, just a little, and rested his chin on the top of her head. 'No, you're staying here and you're going to cry. As long and as hard as you need to. You need to get it out of your system, sweetheart.'

'I can't,' she sobbed, her throat burning as she tried to repress the bubbling emotion.

'Yes, you can, Cal. And you will, because you're not going anywhere.'

She was so tired, tired of holding it back, sick of being brave, of being strong. Crying, *sobbing*, was self-indulgent and useless, but maybe she did need to let go, to release all the emotion she'd kept bottled up for so long.

But whether she wanted to let go or not, there was no stopping the tears. Somehow, she'd released a high-pressure cork, and a loud, guttural sob broke the silence between them. Then another. God, how was she making those weird sounds? A part of her, disconnected from the sobbing woman sitting on Judah's lap, watched her cry, tears dripping from her cheeks and chin onto her hands, turning his light T-shirt a deeper shade of blue.

Judah simply held her and listened to her snort and sob, his grip on her not easing, his support unwavering. After many minutes—five? Ten?—her tears dried up, and her sobs turned to the occasional hiccup. She felt exhausted and empty, and lighter than she had in years. Clean, like she'd taken a mental shower. So that was why people advocated for crying jags. She got it now.

Judah stroked her hair off her damp forehead and dipped his head to look at her. 'Better?' he asked, in the same tone he would use to enquire whether she wanted a cup of coffee.

Calla nodded.

'Can I say something?'

Calla nodded.

He held her face, his fingers on her neck, his

thumb on her jaw. 'I don't think anyone has told you how damn courageous you were, how incredibly strong. Most women would've curled up in a ball and retreated, but not you. You didn't. You kept going, kept fighting. Maybe you were fuelled by rage, but you chose to move forward, to plant your feet. That takes guts and grit, Calla. And I'm so bloody proud of you for choosing to fight rather than flee.'

Compliments weren't something she'd received often, infrequently from her clients, never from Jack. Judah's sincerity was… God, it was *everything*. It made her feel seen, valued and respected.

'Thank you,' she murmured, touched. She'd always remember making love to him in the sunlight, but she'd remember this moment more.

His arms briefly tightened around her, before he released her. 'You must be hot—I know I am.' Still holding her, he swivelled, placed his feet on the floor and easily stood, her in his arms. She instinctively hooked an arm around his neck.

'Where are you taking me?' she asked, tipping her head back to look into his strong, sexy face. She couldn't resist this man anymore, not for a second. And yes, she was falling for him again. Or maybe she'd fallen last year, and she'd simply resumed her spiral. It didn't matter how it happened. Neither did she know how the future would unfold, where they went from here, but she didn't want to let a day pass before she spoke, touched or kissed him again.

Right now, nothing mattered. Not the difference in their ages—so inconsequential—not the fact that she worked for him, not her company or her clients. In this moment and in his arms, there was only Judah and the way he made her feel. Strong, capable, talented, treasured. Seen. So very seen.

Calla was happy to go wherever he led her. But she didn't expect him to walk her into his infinity pool.

CHAPTER NINE

A WEEK LATER, Judah helped Calla out of his doorless Jeep, taking a moment to admire her tanned legs and arms in her thigh-length, short-sleeved brown-and-white-patterned dress. She'd been in St Croix for nearly three weeks now, and she looked so much better than she did when she first arrived. The dark stripes under her eyes were gone, and the frown between her eyebrows had vanished too. She often walked on the beach while he jogged, swam while he surfed, and she was fitter and stronger, her muscles looser.

Whether it was from the sun, sea or the sex, or a combination of all three, she was now quick to smile. The quality of her work had also improved; her designs were more relaxed and a great deal more playful. He'd told her a few days ago that he was happy to go to contract for her to revamp Sol House, but she'd demurred, saying she needed more time to finalise her design, to make it perfect.

His lover, it turned out, was a perfectionist and was never satisfied with 'good enough'.

Outside one of St Croix's best restaurants, tucked inside one of the many eighteenth-century Danish-style buildings that lined Christiansted's cobblestone streets, Calla slid her hand into Judah's and looked up at him. 'It's nice to be out and about. Apparently, this restaurant is fantastic.'

He nodded, taking a moment to scan the street for paparazzi. They rarely bothered him on the island, but he wasn't naive—the locals were curious. Rumours about Calla being his lover were making the rounds, especially within the expat community. The Vegas rule—what happened there, stayed there—applied to St Croix, as well. But he couldn't count on their discretion lasting forever. Eventually, he and Calla would end up in a gossip column. It was unavoidable. He'd ordered his PR team to monitor the situation, and he would know as soon as a story about him and Calla broke.

He glanced at Calla, so small next to him. Should he drop her hand? Then again, why the hell shouldn't he hold it? They were both single, both consenting adults. They weren't breaking the law. Yet he still, before following Calla into the restaurant—a tiny thirty-seater serving divine food—looked up and down the street one more time. Why did he feel like he was being watched?

He shook his head. He was being paranoid.

Judah greeted the owner, introduced her to Calla and stood back as the two women chatted about the restaurant and Crucian food. When she was relaxed, Calla was quietly charming and sweet.

Judah followed Calla and the hostess to their table, pulled out her seat and waited for her to settle before taking his own. Calla ordered chardonnay, and he asked for a beer. David had been a lifelong teetotaller and preached against alcohol, but Judah enjoyed the occasional beer, whiskey or glass of wine. He was, however, careful about sending the wrong message to his customers and rarely drank in public. But he was in St Croix, on holiday, and…*sod it*. It was a beer, not a line of cocaine.

'You're mulling something,' Calla said, pulling his attention back to her. Her hair was in a loose plait, pulled to one side, and it hung over one shoulder. She wore minimal make-up—she didn't need much—and she'd swapped out her normal gold hoop earrings for a long earring falling in a long, smooth sparkle to her shoulder.

'You look lovely, by the way.'

He loved how pink stained her cheek bones when he complimented her.

'Thank you. You seem a little distracted. Is everything okay?'

She was the only one who could see through his mask of implacability. And he still found it unsettling. He gestured to his ear. 'I like your earring thing,' he said. 'And the way you've done your hair.'

She narrowed her eyes, waved his words away and leaned her forearms on the table. 'Thank you, again. Now stop trying to change the subject, and tell me what you're thinking about,' she said, her eyes locked on his.

He might be marginally better at opening up than she was—neither of them found baring their souls easy—but he did want to run his thoughts about Reyes Luxe past her. He never did that with anyone else, not even his most trusted employees. But he knew he could trust Calla. She wasn't the type to blab.

'I decided not to buy ForgeRitual,' he told her. Without engaging with the board or even reading their written demand, he'd issued an internal statement ditching the project and instructing everyone to move on. To say the board wasn't pleased was an understatement. 'I need to start coalescing my vision for the company, where I want to take it, and what I want to focus on. I'm thinking of taking it in a new direction and doing a complete rebrand.'

She placed her chin in the centre of her palm, her attention wholly on him. He liked it. 'Tell me more.'

Could he? Should he? He waited while the waitress delivered their drinks, and when she walked away, and after they'd clinked glasses, he spoke again. 'I've also realised I'm not happy with our core message,' he said.

'Which is?' Calla asked.

'That health is everything, and if it's not your everything, you're wrong and ignorant.'

Calla shook her head. 'I think you are being a bit harsh, Jude.'

He loved it when she shortened his name; nobody else ever had. It warmed him and made him feel more connected, and made it easier to talk to her. She wasn't only his lover, but his friend. Possibly his best friend.

'What comes to mind when you think about Reyes Luxe?' he asked.

'Mm,' she murmured. 'I think of wealth, that it's an exclusive club of glossy, fit people who have the time and money to spend at the gym, at spas and at wellness centres.'

'Exactly.' He took a sip of his beer. 'And I think that's what I'm struggling with, the glossy, the wealth. And the idea that you have to be fit and gorgeous and rich to be a part of the Reyes Luxe world.'

She pursed her lips, thinking. 'If you wanted to take the company in another direction, it would mean an entire rebrand of the company, Judah. Part of its appeal is that it's aspirational, that it's for golden people and that you, as a client, are part of an elite club.'

She was so smart, and he liked that about her. Judah took a sip of his beer and scratched an itch on his cheek. 'Did you know that my dad only got into the health and wellness industry because of my mum?' he asked.

She shook her head, her eyes on his face. All of her attention was on him, and he loved it. Loved the way their eyes connected, the way her fingers occasionally brushed the side of his hand, grounding him and reminding him of the physical connection they shared.

'She was a runway model, but into alternative health, organic foods, walking barefoot and communing with nature. A complete free spirit.' He smiled. 'My mum was a punk rocker activist with the soul of a sixties flower child.'

Calla gifted him with a soft and sweet smile. 'I love that.'

'Apparently, when they first met, my dad was overweight, completely stressed out and he never exercised. My mum changed his diet, got him exercising, and he lost the weight, and he got fit. Then very fit, and his weight and how he looked became an obsession. Reyes Luxe was born from his "transformation".'

Judah looked out of the window, saw a man standing in a doorway opposite, dressed in black pants and jeans. He frowned. Who wore black on a summer's evening in the Caribbean? He turned his attention back to Calla. 'It's ironic that my two health-obsessed parents, obsessed in completely different ways, both died from what the experts call the scourges of modern-day life, cancer and a heart attack.'

'It happens more often than we like to think to super-fit people.' She leaned back in her chair and rested her hands in her lap. 'While I love hearing about your parents and would like to know more, we've veered off the subject of Reyes Luxe. Tell me about the new direction and Reyes Luxe's rebrand.'

It was his first time putting his thoughts into words and, ridiculously, he felt a little nervous. 'I feel like I've been wearing someone else's shoes for months now. I think it's time I kicked them off.' Calla didn't look surprised, she simply nodded, her expression encouraging him to continue. 'But it would be stupid to shrug off the Reyes Luxe brand entirely, too much work and money has gone into making it what it is. But I'm considering making it smaller, even more exclusive, more expensive.'

As he expected, her brow furrowed. ‘That’s not what I expected you to say. Aren’t you trying to get away from the glitz and glam?’

He nodded. ‘Yes and no. If I’m going to cater to the rich, then I’m going to target the very rich and market only to them, through exclusive channels. I’m going to make Reyes Luxe products exceptionally high-end and exceptionally exclusive. That’ll make the line *exceptionally* profitable. I’m going to only have one Reyes Luxe spa and club per city instead of many, and I’m going to make them extremely difficult to access. It’ll be the club every rich person wants to join but can’t.’

People loved what they couldn’t easily access, and he knew he’d have no problem with the concept or upping the price of the membership to stratospheric levels.

‘But you own multiple clubs, spas and wellness centres. What are you going to do with those buildings?’

He’d given this a lot of thought. ‘I’m going to turn them into family-friendly, easily accessible and fun to visit facilities. I’m going to launch a new brand of wellness centres, gyms and spas with new and revamped premises. And I’m going to establish an affordable health line that will appeal to a wider swathe of the population. That feels…’

Calla tipped her head to the side, waiting for him to continue. He rubbed the back of his neck. 'That feels authentic to me, Cal.'

She didn't speak for a beat, maybe two. 'Are you waiting for my input, Judah?'

He nodded. Of course he was, her opinion meant more to him than all his senior management, his board members. She got him, like no one ever had.

'May I ask why?'

It was time to get honest, to call it like it was, to be who he was. Maybe he'd flame out, but all he could do was try. Because if he wasn't living true to his values, what was the point? He was sick of one-night stands, of casual couplings, a dinner here and there, working sixteen-hour days for something he didn't, wholly, believe in, pocketing money he didn't need. He wanted conversations with Calla, deep, light and everything in between, her in his bed, some sort of future, preferably one that resulted in babies, chaos and cohabiting.

'Because when I looked up and took stock of my life and tried to work out when last I felt like myself, I pinpointed it to that weekend I spent with you. And having you back in my life, and in my bed, feels real and right.'

She gripped her bottom lip with her teeth,

worry in her eyes. He knew she was about to backpedal. Three, two, one…

'I don't know if I'm there, Judah. I'm not sure if I can give you what you want.' She linked her hands together, and they turned white with pressure. 'I'm not good with trust, Judah, you know this. And you know why.'

He leaned forward, his eyes locked on her. 'I am *not* your ex, Calla.' Her expression turned blank, and a curtain came down in her eyes. Dammit, he didn't want to argue with her. He'd planned on having a romantic evening, some good food, better wine, a walk along the beach before heading home and taking her to bed. They'd moved off Reyes Luxe and somehow skated into a patch of thorns. Should he retreat or should he face this head on? If he backed down, it would only raise its head later on, so he might as well forge forward. But he knew the chances of a romantic walk and a night of hot sex were rapidly dropping.

He raked his hand through his hair. 'Look, I'm not asking you to make a for life commitment here, I'm just telling you that this goes beyond sex for me.'

Calla pushed the tips of her fingers into her forehead. 'Judah, half in and half out, second-guessing everything, and being in limbo doesn't work for me. I need boundaries, boxes, a plan, to be in control. I need a safety net.' She held up her hand. 'And don't tell me you can be that for me!'

She bit down hard on her lip. 'Look, I can't… not *yet*.'

He heard her unspoken words…*maybe not ever*. There was no point pushing her, so he opted to change the subject. 'Shall we eat first and postpone this?'

'No.' Right, her short response wasn't a surprise. 'You obviously have some strong opinions on this, so please carry on.'

He sighed. 'You're hiding away, scared to engage, make a move, be happy, because he was such a dick. You're giving him too much power over you.'

'I'm trying to protect my business,' she stated, her words as pointed as the business end of a fencing sword. 'To regroup and rebuild.'

'I'm not talking about your business or what you do at work, I'm talking about *you*. You're trying to protect yourself. And I hate that you think you have to protect yourself from me, that you have painted us with the same brush.'

'I haven't—'

'You won't take a chance on me, on us, on whatever is bubbling between us because of him. That's lumping me with him.' And he goddamn hated it.

'That's not fair,' she hissed, her hand gripping

the linen serviette and crumpling it into a tight ball. 'I'm also your client and there are six years between us.'

Oh, now she was clutching at straws. His temper started to simmer, but he immediately dialled it down. 'Using our age difference is a B.S. excuse, Calla, and beneath you.'

She flushed, embarrassed, but she still met his eyes. 'You're right, that was beneath me.'

And there it was, one more thing he liked about her. She was quick to apologise and didn't sulk. Nor did she hold grudges. Calla gripped the bridge of her nose with her index finger and thumb and closed her eyes. 'I'm trying, Judah, I *am*.'

He sat back and picked up his glass, draining his beer in one long swallow. 'Are you, Calla? I don't think you are. I think you're pretty comfortable in your emotional suit of armour—you like it there.' Seeing her expression, he curled his fingers around hers, happy she didn't pull away as he expected her to. 'You've got that stubborn look on your face. You feel like I am pushing you.'

She nodded. 'Yes, I do.'

'I am. Someone has to, Calla. And it looks like that somebody is me.'

He'd given her enough to think about, so Judah picked up a menu, wanting to move on and salvage their evening. 'Let's decide what we want to eat and then we'll talk about something else.'

Calla's relief was so obvious he nearly smiled. She liked to skirt emotions, to play it safe. He wasn't prepared to let her do that for much longer. They placed their order—fresh fish for her, kallaloo for him—and Judah topped up her wine glass from the chilly bottle resting in the ice bucket next to their table.

'Talking about business, before we left the house, I signed your electronic contract and paid your deposit.' He watched as his words settled, as excitement turned her chinks pink and put fireworks in her eyes. 'I'd like you to start work renovating my house as soon as possible.'

'Really?'

Their disagreement was forgotten, and excitement rolled off her. 'Really.' He lifted a teasing eyebrow, his mouth lifting in a smile he couldn't contain. 'What? You didn't think I brought you to a fantastic restaurant only because I'm crazy about you and want to figure out where we go from here? I have to be able to write this off as a business expense, you know.'

Calla laughed, balled up her linen serviette and threw it at his head. She leaned forward, picked the cloth off his shoulder, and her eyes filled with laughter. 'You liked them, right? My designs?' she asked, vibrating.

That was easy to answer. 'I adore your designs.' *I adore you.*

It was her turn to lift a naughty, suggestive eyebrow. 'Then do you think your expense account will stretch to a bottle of champagne?'

Later that evening, Calla lay facing Judah on his extra-wide, extra-long bed. Through the open window, the moon tossed shadows on his face as it played peekaboo with the clouds. His hand lay heavy on her hip, and she lifted her finger to lightly, softly, trace the arch of his right eyebrow, before sliding it down his cheek and across his stubbled jaw. She was perfectly content lying here looking at him and suspected that she would be happy to pass most of her nights this way. But she couldn't think straight when she lay this close to him, and she desperately needed to make sense of what she was thinking and feeling.

Calla lifted his hand to place it on the empty space next to him. 'Don't go, Cal,' he muttered, in a growly, saturated-with-sleep voice. For tonight or forever? Both were tempting...

Calla slipped out of his bed, pulled on his shirt and picked up the half-empty bottle of champagne on the bedside table. They'd brought the expensive bottle back to bed with them, but as soon as their clothes started to fly, heads and hearts raced, and the expensive liquor was forgotten. Taking a sip, she carried it out onto the balcony and leaned back against the bedroom wall, feeling like she was hovering somewhere between the sea and the stars. A bit shaky, she slid down the wall and sat down.

Calla took in the sea beyond the tempered glass barrier, a part of her wishing it wasn't such a gorgeous night. Thoughts like hers, complicated and chaotic, deserved thunder and lightning, or fog, something that matched her mood. Not a warm, fragrant night with stars that glittered and gleamed, sparkly celestial fruit hanging low in the sky.

Having you back in my life, and my bed, feels real, and right.

Doubts, hot and hard, rolled through her. While she was so excited about renovating Sol House—and the opportunities it afforded her for bigger and better projects—on a personal level, she was terrified at how fast her and Judah's relationship was moving. She lifted the champagne bottle to her lips, her head whirling. Judah had asked too much of her and pushed too hard. He was being unreasonable. Who made life-changing decisions after just a few weeks? Who changed the way they lived their life, did a complete one-eighty because of some lovely conversations and good sex? He was asking for too much, too soon. Assuming too much...

Seeing too much.

But, dammit, they were great together. They just worked. She had the creative flair, he had a brain for numbers, but they were intellectual equals, and their conversations covered a wide range of subjects. They could discuss politics over breakfast, argue about organised religion over dinner and then fall into bed, completely in sync, giving and taking pleasure.

His comment about her measuring him against Jack had landed like a gut punch—mostly because, deep down, she knew he wasn't wrong. Calla placed her fist into her sternum, trying to will the burn away. Why did it have to hurt? She thought she was over being hurt by anything Jack-related.

She'd believed she'd built enough walls to keep the hurt out. But here she was—reeling from Judah's words, stung by truths she didn't want to face, little burrs she couldn't shake. And damn it, they hurt because they were true. *'Hiding', 'scared', 'you've given up your power'.*

She winced and shoved her hands into her hair, tugging on the strands. She wished she could discount his words, brush them off, but that was impossible. Judah was important to her, had been from the moment they first connected last year. But did she value him enough, care about him—love him?—enough to take a chance, to change?

What was she prepared to give up to be with Judah?

Along with being hypervigilant about her reputation, she'd been determined to control every aspect of her life and had vowed never to give up her independence, to let another man control her again. After what Jack did to her, she was allowed to feel that way, to protect herself.

And yes, maybe she did associate emotional vulnerability with humiliation and powerlessness, and still believed survival, emotional and financial, depended on never relying on anyone again. And for the first time, she admitted it—she was still carrying so much shame. For falling for Jack. For letting him twist her mind and heart. For handing over her heart like a fool and pretending she didn't see the cracks forming, for letting him get away with treating her like trash. And while she was admitting uncomfortable truths…

Judah was right when he said she'd painted him with the same brush, that she was judging him by what her ex-husband did. And that, God…that wasn't fair. Or right. Judah was the antithesis of her ex, someone who'd never once made her feel less than, powerless or unseen. He listened when she spoke, considered her opinions; sometimes agreeing with her, sometimes not. But he respected her right to have them. He valued her work and frequently complimented what she did and how she approached a subject or a problem. And when he disagreed with her, he kept his tone respectful, his attitude open. She wasn't his punching bag, a way to make himself feel better, or there to prop up his ego.

Judah saw her as an equal, an adult. There would never be one set of rules for him, another for her. Their relationship would be a partnership; sometimes he would lead, sometimes she'd step up to the plate. There would be times when she'd pull him through a rough patch, and he'd do the same for her. They'd be a team, and they'd operate on a level playing field. Could she do it?

Calla looked at the dark sea beyond the transparent balcony. The moon peeked out from the clouds, its silvery light turning the sea's surface to the same deep blue as Judah's eyes. Could she live without his eyes on her? She didn't think so. And if she didn't take this second chance Fate was offering her, would she regret it for the rest of her life? Yes, she thought she would.

But that meant being brave, fighting against her instinct to retreat, to hide behind her suit of emotional armour, as Judah called it. She would have to gather every bit of courage she possessed and go to Judah, suggesting they take the next (baby) steps. What those were, she wasn't sure. Maybe just admitting she was prepared to try was the first step on what she knew might be a long journey.

But she wasn't alone. As Judah said, he'd be there every step of the way. And she believed he meant it.

And that was everything, wasn't it?

CHAPTER TEN

THE NEXT MORNING, Judah looked at the message he received from his head of his PR department, stunned at what he was seeing. On his screen was a photo of him and Calla, taken yesterday outside the restaurant in Christiansted. His hand rested low on her back, his head bent to listen to her, an affectionate smile on his face. Calla's expression was even more revealing; her eyes sparkled, and her smile wide and sexy.

Everyone with a brain in their head could tell their relationship went far beyond the professional.

Judah released a long, desperate curse and scowled at the headline. Calla West, Cougar Designer, Snags Billionaire Heir.

Seriously? *What the actual...*? He ran his hand through his hair and walked from his study onto the wraparound patio of his master suite and looked down. On the entertainment deck below him, Calla sat on the edge of a lounger under the shade of an umbrella, her attention on the tablet resting on her knee and her phone plastered to her ear. She'd been quiet earlier when they parted ways for the day ahead, not sulky but introspective. Judah suspected she was working through their conversation, trying to process what he said about her ex and her emotional armour. He was happy to give her time to think; he wanted Calla to come to him, warm and willing and optimistic about the future.

But this article would hit her like an emotional napalm strike, and because of who he was, it would go viral—if it hadn't already. That was the world they lived in. Judah rubbed the back of his neck, frustrated. Why hadn't he trusted his instincts when he thought someone was watching them? Why hadn't he kept Calla at home instead of exposing her to someone's photo lens and vitriolic pen? Why hadn't he considered all the consequences of them being seen in public?

And while he was at it, maybe he could try thinking a little more and talking a little less when it came to their relationship? Approach the situation with more caution instead of acting like a bull caught between a matador and an escape route?

What was wrong with him?

Judah rested his forearms on the toughened glass walls, his eyes on Calla's head. The implications in the article were vicious, and the timing, just a day after she announced she'd landed the commission to renovate Sol House on social media, was highly suspect. It wasn't just bad press, it was a character assassination. Against a woman who'd already rebuilt herself from scratch. Judah had no doubt her ex was behind it...

What could he do? How could he crush the cockroach? His PR department back in the UK was already doing what they could to negate the impact of the article. But spin could only go so far and had a limited effect; the internet was a powerful beast and not easily contained or corralled.

Once the shock wore off, how would she take it? What would she do next? He didn't know—and that uncertainty scared the hell out of him. Judah shivered, suddenly cold. Unfortunately, he didn't have much faith she'd be able to shrug it off. As he'd said earlier, her wounds were deep and she'd never allowed them to heal.

This might split them wide open again.

Later that day, Calla knocked on the doorframe to Judah's study. It took a moment for him to raise his head, for his eyes to focus on her leaning against the door-frame. She still wasn't used to seeing him wearing glasses, and she smiled, thinking he rocked the look. Sexy and studious, a killer combination. Judah pulled the black frames off his face and tossed them onto his desk. He leaned back in his chair and gestured for her to come inside.

'Hi. I was just finishing up and I was going to come find you, but you beat me to it.' He pushed back his chair and walked around the desk to stand in front of her. 'Are you okay?'

She reached out to grab his shirt, twisting the cotton fabric between her fingers, before stroking it smooth, leaving her hand on his chest. God, she loved touching him. 'Mm, I'm fine. I've been doing a lot of thinking, and I'm better than I thought I would be.'

She felt some tension leave his body, a little surprised he was still worried about their discussion last night. Did he think she was fragile? He hadn't yelled at her, nor had he been nasty; he'd simply, clearly and calmly, stated his thoughts. Sure, they'd been hard to hear, but that didn't mean he was wrong. She still had things to work through, some old habits to discard, but she'd decided to make some changes, to explore this second shot at something special.

Calla rested her forehead against his chest and gripped his sides, feeling the warmth of his skin beneath the thin cotton of his shirt. 'I thought you would be on either your surf or paddleboard, not sitting in your office.'

'I wanted to stick around, to keep an eye on you, see how you were doing.' He lifted his hand to stroke her hair. 'You're taking this a lot better than I thought. I've been so worried about you.'

It was sweet of him to care so much about a small argument. Jack never worried about her; her feelings never registered with him. In Judah, she'd found a man completely opposite to her waste-of-space ex. He actually cared about her, cared about what she was thinking and feeling. It felt both strange and completely wonderful. She snuggled into him, her arms tightening around his lower back. She didn't know how they were going to make this work, but she wanted to spend the rest of her life in his arms.

'I'd love to explore other restaurants in Christiansted or, well, anywhere with you. Maybe we could skip the minor argument next time?'

Judah's grip tightened, and tension slid into him. Calla frowned and pulled back. She tipped her head back and took in his confused expression. 'Why are you looking so serious?' she asked. 'Did the restaurant burn down or something?'

He stroked her arm and stepped back, resting his butt on his wide desk. 'You're here to talk about our conversation last night?'

She spread her hands. Well, yes. What else

was there to talk about? 'I've been thinking about what you said and maybe it's time for me to—'

'Nobody sent you the link?' he asked, abruptly interrupting her.

'What are you talking about, Judah?' she asked, scared by his sombre expression and the hesitation in his eyes.

'I would've thought one of your people would've kept you up-to-date.'

Her people? She employed three designers on an ad-hoc basis, and she was her own secretary, accountant, promoter and scheduler. She was *it*. She hadn't been able to afford permanent staff since she lost her half of Atelier Abernathy.

'I don't have people, Judah. I'm a one-man band,' she explained. 'What link and what are you talking about?'

He pushed his hand through his hair, his lips a thin slash in his face. He dropped an F-bomb and reached back to pick up his phone. 'I thought you were here to talk about this.'

He activated face recognition, then held the phone out for her to take. Calla frowned, her heart thumping against her ribs. She hesitated, instinctively fighting the urge to run. Whatever he wanted her to look at would, she knew, change everything.

It took her a while to look down. It took her even longer to make sense of the headline.

Calla West, Cougar Designer, Snags Billionaire Heir.

She skimmed the article, just enough to catch the gut punches and for the words to form ice crystals in her blood.

In St Croix to renovate his house, she has moved into his bedroom.

Did she use time-tested techniques to secure future projects?

Was once married to celebrity designer Jack Abernathy of Atelier Abernathy.

Her eyes tripped over the words, and she had to, once or twice, go back to read a sentence again. It was clever, in the way poison often was—a sprinkling of truth and just enough innuendo to make people think her and Judah's association was...dirty. There was nothing explicitly false; the truth was hidden behind layers of supposition and just enough to make the article credible. It was clever, but supremely ugly, journalism.

Her brain stalled. Her breath too. She was in

a tunnel, wind howling through it—icy, sharp, bitter—carrying her old friend, panic, betrayal and shame.

She couldn't breathe.

The article's photo took up half the screen, high-res and unmistakably her. Her head thrown back, laughing up at Judah, his hand proprietary on her back. That damned dress—she'd loved it up until a few minutes ago. She'd loved how she'd felt in it. Confident, sexy, so feminine. Alive.

They looked like a couple sharing an inside joke, like the kind of couple who didn't have to try too hard. Like she was…*his.* She'd been cold a few seconds ago, but now an intense heat hit her in waves—jagged and rising. Her lungs tightened, and her vision blurred at the edges. She staggered back, bile lacing her throat, her stomach threatening to revolt. She swallowed it down.

Lie after lie, coated in just enough truth. But that wasn't even the worst part. The worst part was how familiar it all felt. How awful it felt to have her work and personal life collide, how helpless she felt to watch everything she'd worked so hard for evaporate. The reputation she'd tried to restore, the long hours, the way she'd hustled meant nothing. Thanks to this article, it had been a complete waste of her time and energy.

It didn't matter that she'd handed Judah an amazing design, that she'd perfectly interpreted—after a few rough starts—what he wanted. That her renderings were flawless, and that he'd signed off on her work with a satisfied grin and a 'damn, you nailed it'.

She'd worked harder than she ever had in her life—because it was Judah. And because her pride demanded that she do her best, give him all she had, because she never wanted anyone, especially him, to think she'd slacked off because of their history and their previous and personal connection. What mattered—what always seemed to matter—was the story. And this article insinuated she'd set out to seduce Judah, that she'd slept with him for this, and future, contracts. Just like Jack always hinted before, during and after their divorce; it was an essential part of his smear campaign. It was always tucked between the insinuations that she was 'emotional', 'unreliable' and 'unbalanced.' It was his way of continuously reminding the world that she was unworthy and not to be trusted.

She knew how this would play out. The Reyes Luxe board would see the article, and she'd be painted as a liability. The people in Judah's PR department would curse her from here to Sunday. Judah would be asked—no, pressured—to distance himself. He'd pay the penalty clause to terminate her contract, because having her out of his life, and house, would be easier. So much cleaner. And it was just like Jack wanted.

As for her…

The calls enquiring whether she'd be interested in design projects would stop coming, the emails would dry up and the whispers and rumours, fed by Jack, would spread. Clients, future and present, would hear of Judah pulling out, and they'd boycott her. *'Check her out, she's the one who couldn't hold onto her marriage or business. And, apparently, Judah Reyes.'*

'That's what happens when you think you can fly close to the sun.'

'It's rumoured she can't manage her emotions.'

'She's unstable.'

Unworthy.

And every woman in the industry who'd clawed her way up without compromising her ethics would view her as the poster girl for sleeping her way into the spotlight. A million fire ants crawled under her skin.

'Calla, say something,' Judah's voice sliced through the silence, sharp with worry.

She blinked, looked at him, then down at his

phone. That picture of them, intimate and connected, mocked her.

'What's there to say?' she whispered.

'It's bullshit,' he insisted.

She met his eyes, heart pounding like it was trying to break free of her chest. 'You think that matters?' she asked quietly. 'Do you honestly think truth beats perception? That talent beats gossip?'

Judah looked furious. And—God help her—unsure, like he didn't know what to do or how to help. But all she could feel was fear. A full-body, spine-deep panic.

Judah stepped forward, his hands coming to her arms. She wrenched back. '*Don't.*'

'Calla...'

'This always happens,' she said, her voice cracking. 'I let myself feel safe. With you. And look where it got me.'

He flinched like she'd hit him. 'I didn't do this.'

It should matter, but she couldn't let it. 'I let you in. And now I'm the woman I promised myself I'd never be again.'

'You're just you and the article is garbage,' Judah said again, voice low, intense. 'It doesn't change anything.'

'It changes *everything*.' Her voice rose, sharp with panic. 'Don't you get it? This isn't just PR for me, Judah. This is my *life*. My reputation. My future. You can survive this, I can't.

'I need to go,' she said, stepping back, heart breaking with every inch of distance. 'I should never have stayed this long. I should've got to work sooner, worked harder and smarter. I knew better than to mix business and pleasure.'

His expression twisted, like he wanted to argue. But she couldn't afford to let him talk, because she ached to believe this was survivable. It wasn't. 'Do you think that walking away fixes this?' he asked, frustrated.

Nothing could fix the pain, the landslide of devastation sliding through her heart. 'No.' Her voice softened. 'But it's what I know how to do.'

Because if she stayed, she'd start leaning on him. And that was a risk she couldn't take. Not again. Judah would tend to her wounds, talk her down and patch her up. He was a protector and a white knight, he lived to make people feel better. But the patches peeled and the painkillers wore off. Eventually, those wounds would open up again, and she'd start bleeding again.

It would be a never-ending cycle of waiting for the pain to return.

So she steeled herself, turned and walked away. It wasn't because she didn't care, but because she cared too much.

And the next time they saw or spoke to each

other—she needed to know what he intended to do about her contract to revamp his house—he'd get the version of her with walls so high, no one could scale them. She'd be professional. Cold. Controlled.

Everything she should've been and wasn't.

Calla rested her head against the rim of the plane's window and stared into the clouds below the wing of the aircraft. Her heart already ached to be back in St Croix, to be with Judah, but that wasn't an option.

She was back where she was before...no, she was many steps behind. Calla banged her head, a part of her wishing he'd never contacted her. She could've just kept chugging along in New York City, taking on one project at a time, chipping away at Jack's influence on their industry. But she'd been ambitious, and she'd wanted more.

And because she'd mixed business and pleasure, look where she was now. Her reputation was shredded, more tarnished than it was before, and Judah, she was sure, was regretting bringing her to the island and handing her the commission to revamp Sol House.

Oh, she'd received a few messages from him—she was ignoring his calls—and he talked a good game, saying that he still wanted her as his designer and his lover. But Calla knew that in a few days, when the dust settled and the distance between them widened, his sharp, strategic brain would kick in. When that happened, he'd appreciate her leaving, for removing herself calmly and quietly from his life. He'd realise that being with her meant facing more attacks like this from Jack, and that he'd be caught up in all the nastiness her ex could, and would, generate.

He'd soon realise he'd had a lucky escape.

Jack, dammit, was so clever. She did not doubt that the photograph and its accompanying article were his work. By implying she'd used sex to win Judah's high-profile project was confirmation bias for everyone who'd listened when he disparaged her. It was validation that she relied on manipulation instead of talent and hard work. So many people, ex-clients, current clients, industry heavyweights, would now believe she didn't earn this project—she'd seduced it.

She'd clung to the idea that she could go up against Jack and his family, that through hard work, grit and producing excellent designs, she could rehabilitate her reputation. That, with one high-profile client, she could reclaim her name, brand and reputation. It was stunning to realise that she could still be so naive. But, because she'd been blinded by the urge to get ahead, to take the next step, she'd ignored her instinct to leave St Croix after discovering Judah was her client. And when their attraction flared hot and bright, she convinced herself she could keep their professional and personal lives separate. Hah! What a joke. They'd collided spectacularly.

With Judah, she'd lost the control she'd clung to like a life ring in a stormy sea. She'd allowed her boundaries to be obliterated and her feelings for him—written on her face and captured by that photograph—were out there for the world to see, oh-so visible.

She'd let her walls be washed away by laughter and fantastic sex, by easy conversations and St Croix's summer breeze. Worst of all, she forgot that the best predictor of the future was the past. She'd let someone in and lost everything again.

She'd never allow that to happen again. And this time her words were cast in stone.

She'd walked away. *Again.*

Judah stood next to the infinity pool, his hip against the balustrade, utterly confounded. He'd expected a fight, tears, for them to scrap and scramble their way through this, but she'd just packed her stuff and bolted. What the hell?

No dramatic pause, no glance over her shoulder. She'd just turned and went, oblivious to the fact that she'd cracked his chest open and taken his heart with her. Calla walking away gutted him in ways he didn't expect. He'd let himself believe that instinct might be enough—that maybe he didn't need every answer or a polished plan to be worthy of love, to be the leader of Reyes Luxe, to enjoy the life and wealth he'd inherited. She made him feel like it was okay to like and trust himself again. And now she was gone.

And the old, gnawing fear—that he wasn't enough, not for her, not for the company, not for this life handed to him before he was ready—was back, simmering under the surface. Calla had quieted his doubts for a while, but with her gone, they were back, louder than before.

The sea rolled up on the rocks, liquid and lazy, and the sky blazed blue. The sun still shone, and everyone on the island carried on, but Judah simply stood there, motionless. Numb. Honestly, it would've been so much easier if she'd left because she was a gold-digger, or if he'd caught her with someone else, if she'd been mean and selfish and annoying. But she'd been, dammit, well, not perfect, but for the little time they'd spent together, perfect for him.

He couldn't help but pull out his phone and find the picture he'd saved from that article, staring at it as if he could mentally will her back to St Croix. She looked so radiant, open, and so herself. He looked a little dopey, completely under her spell, like she hung the damn moon.

They looked happy. But someone, her ex, he presumed, took whatever the hell they had—they hadn't even had time to define it properly—and weaponised it. That was unforgivable. He shoved his phone back into his pocket, dragged both hands over his face, and sat down hard on the edge of a lounger.

She thought this couldn't be recovered from. That it was the end. That he'd take the easy way out and allow her to fade from her life. That he'd let her ex have the last word. Well, screw that. And screw his insecurities. He wasn't allowing them a seat at his table.

Calla probably believed he'd cut his losses, minimise the damage and move on. He had no doubt she thought he'd treat her, and what they had, as a mistake. Hadn't she heard him when he told her she was the first real thing in his life since his father died? Okay, maybe he hadn't clearly explained how she brought colour, spark and goddamn soul back into his world.

But that's how he felt.

And he never walked away from something he wanted, never ran away from a fight. God, why hadn't she planted her feet, and stayed, fought instead of fleeing?

They had something—it had been there ten

months ago, and was bigger and brighter now. And he *wanted* her. Not because she'd do an amazing job revamping his house, or for the work she did. Or because she was an amazing lover and set his blood on fire.

She was, simply, the best thing, then and now, that ever happened to him. Because she saw him. Because she made him feel whole.

And now she was gone, all because some parasitic rag splattered her insecurities and fears all over the 'net. God, the look on her face when she read the article…like it confirmed every terrible thing she'd ever been told, all that she'd been taught to believe about herself.

And the knife through his soul?

Being away from normal life, caught up in her and the way she made him feel, he'd forgotten he was Judah Reyes. He hadn't seen the article coming and hadn't protected her from it. He was used to media storms. He knew how to play that game—shrug, smile, deny, distract. But this wasn't just another PR flare-up, a passing storm. This was Calla's *life*. Her career. Her name.

Judah pushed the heels of his hands into his eye sockets, wishing that she'd trusted him more with her wounds, with her battered soul. Had he understood, really understood, how deep her cuts were, he would've held her so damn carefully.

But he hadn't, and she'd run. And this time, he

didn't think she'd come back. If she did, for the sake of renovating his house, she'd be wrapped up in layers of professionalism and pride. He leaned forward, elbows on his knees, staring at the sleepy sea like it held his answers in its blue depths. His jaw locked, breath struggling up his tight throat, heart low and sore in his chest.

He could go after her; he could easily track her down. He was a guy who could find some words and say something big, sweeping and heartfelt.

But Calla didn't need to be rescued by him. She wanted, *needed*, to rescue herself. Wasn't everything she'd done since leaving her marriage centred around that belief? She simply wanted to stand in her own space, seen for her talent and her incredible work ethic. She wanted truth. Security. Belief.

But he knew, somehow, from a place deep inside him, that right now all he could give her was space. So Judah forced himself to sit there, his house empty and silent behind him, while the day morphed into night and that damned article kept multiplying across the internet.

He'd let her go. But he wouldn't give her up. Not yet. Not ever.

He knew it before, but it made complete sense to him now. If he was ever going to be the man he wanted to be, authentic, real, grounded, it started and ended with her.

CHAPTER ELEVEN

IT HAD BEEN a hell of a week.

Calla was in her Brooklyn shoebox apartment, eating takeaway and trying not to feel sorry for herself. In a pair of men's boxers and a thin, often washed T-shirt over a sports bra, she sat cross-legged on her sofa, her laptop open but untouched. She'd spent the week reaching out to clients, old, new and potential, and she'd had a few emails back—three, no four—all polite, all unencouraging.

'Regretfully.' 'Temporarily.' 'Given the sensitivity of the situation.'

As she'd thought, she was back to square one, maybe even at minus one. If her life was a snakes and ladders game, she'd be off the board. God, she sounded so damn sorry for herself, and she hated that she did, but this was so hard. So demoralizing. And she missed St Croix…

But more than St Croix, she missed Judah. Missed his half-smile, his deep voice, missed the way he listened to her, like what she had to say was important, like she mattered. And while she was independent and able to look after herself, she did miss how safe she felt in his arms, the feeling she had someone in her corner.

But, damn, when it really mattered, she hadn't let him support her. She'd chosen to run instead. But what other choice did she have? Running, bailing, dropping out—call it what you will—it had been the best thing, the only thing, to do. Nothing else made sense.

Calla's head lifted at the sound of her phone ringing. She frowned and glanced over her shoulder to check the clock on her kitchen wall. It was past ten, too late for a casual or business call.

Annoyed, she stood up and walked over to her desk, looked at her phone and saw the incoming video call from Judah.

She wasn't surprised to hear from him; Judah wasn't someone who'd simply let it end. He wasn't the type to let anything fade away, especially when something mattered to him. And she did.

Her heart bounced off her ribcage as she swiped, and his face filled her screen. Honestly, he looked like hell. His stubble was rougher than usual, his wrinkled shirt open at the collar. Tired, like he hadn't slept properly in days. He also looked—what was the word?—frayed. Calla winced when she caught a glimpse of her face in the small frame in the corner of her phone. Limp hair, white face. Big eyes with blue stripes under them. She looked as rough as he did.

'You shouldn't have called, Judah.' Because how was she supposed to resist him? How could she get used to living without him if he kept showing up?

'Yet I did, and you answered.'

So logical.

Calla sat down on the edge of the couch and waited for him to end the awkward silence, and to explain why he'd called. He just stared at her, hunger in his eyes, and said, 'I needed to check on you.'

That threw her. She gripped her phone tighter. 'Why?'

'Because you matter. Because you're hurting. And I don't want you to do that alone.' Despite the half a second of lag, his concern-filled voice hit her like a wave. Calla swallowed. Her throat ached.

'I'm not some PR mess you can spin. You can't fix me, Judah.'

'I know, and I don't want or need to fix you. You don't *need* fixing.' His voice was quiet, but so sincere. 'I've been doing a lot of thinking, and I think you're a woman who's been dragged through hell by people who thought they had the right to define you. And I'm not going to be another person who does that to you.'

A breath shuddered out of her. How was it that he was always able to see her? To understand? She propped the phone against her laptop screen, too tired to hold it but unable to look away.

'I'm not here about the article, Calla,' he said. 'There are steps I can take… I could issue a statement, push back harder, put my lawyers onto them, and make them hurt. But I'm not going to do that.'

She blinked, trying to make sense of his words.

'And I'm not trying to convince you to stay with me, if you really believe we're better off apart.' His blue eyes didn't waver, his voice was completely calm, and all his focus was on her. 'But I am going to say something I should've said in St Croix.'

She didn't speak. She couldn't; her tongue had lost the ability to form words.

'Firstly, you're a great designer, and I loved your vision for Sol House. I gave you that contract because it's how I want my house to look. It had nothing to do with us.'

She'd learned to read his eyes and knew he spoke the truth. But she'd never doubted his ability to separate work and romance. She'd never doubted him. She was the one with issues.

'That's work. As for how I feel about you as a woman…' His expression remained steady, his eyes didn't leave hers. 'I didn't fall for you because of a one-night stand ten months ago or because we still have the same insane chemistry. I fell for you, back then and now, because you are sharp and stubborn and talented as hell. Because, right from the beginning, I saw you for who you are and what you stand for—I believe you and believe *in* you. You also made me believe in myself and what I was doing and made me understand that I'm allowed to step away from my dad's legacy. You made me want to build something that mattered.'

Calla closed her eyes, her chest still aching.

'I don't care what some trashy headline says,' Judah continued. 'I know who you are. And if the world doesn't see it, then sod them.'

Calla's voice cracked when she finally spoke. 'It's not just the world, Judah. It's me. I see it. That version of me. That woman in the article.' Her mouth twisted. 'And it makes me feel small. Like I've spent too much time dragging myself out of the mud only to fall face-first back in.'

'You didn't fall,' he said, voice like gravel and heat. 'You were pushed. And I get it—you don't want to need anyone. But needing someone isn't weakness, Calla. It's real. It's human.

'I want you,' he continued. 'Not for the project. Not because of our history. Just…you. As you are. Fear and fury and brilliance and all.'

Calla blinked fast, vision blurring. Her armour wavered, then cracked. But it didn't shatter. She wouldn't let it.

Despite the miles between them, his slow, intense smile caressed her. 'I'd love you to see yourself as I see you, as a woman who's strong and bold and courageous. But I can't do that for you—no one can. It's up to you what you do next, Calla. Are you going to believe Jack's version of you, or mine?'

His question ripped through her. She wanted to scream that it wasn't that simple, that people didn't just shed the skin of who they used to be. She'd spent years protecting herself, learning not to need anyone, not to trust. And yet here was Judah, offering something different. Something terrifying. Not a rescue, but complete understanding.

Oh, God, it was too much. 'Judah…'

He shook his head, his eyes warm, full of love. 'That's enough for now, Calla. Just know I'm waiting for you, whenever you're ready. I loved you back then, and I love you now. And I will love you more tomorrow.'

God, it would be so easy to reach for him, to beg him to fly over or to tell him she'd be on the first flight she could find. To run to him, to lose herself in him, in the hope that he could make everything she was wrestling with disappear. But that would be another cop-out. And if she went to him now, without figuring out who she was for once and for all, she'd only lose herself again.

She bit her lip as she held his gaze as he lifted his hand to sign off, her chest tight and her throat raw. When he was gone, she kept staring at the now-blank screen.

He was right.

Before she could be part of them, she needed to know who she was. To stand tall, to not bend, to be a better version of herself.

Not for Judah, but for herself.

Calla had snuck out of enough Abernathy parties over the years to know exactly how to slip into this one. The Fourth of July bash in the Hamptons was exactly as she remembered: tasteful red, white, and blue decor, the scent of overpriced flowers in the air, and a guest list carefully chosen of the wealthy, influential and powerful. She stood on the terrace for a moment, taking it all in—the champagne flutes, the air-kissed greetings, the casually bored mix of investors, designers and editors. And society journalists whose sole job was to report on how wonderful they all were.

She descended the stone steps and crossed the manicured lawn, surprisingly unbothered by the fact that she hadn't been invited and didn't belong. Her sleeveless forest green jumpsuit wasn't designer, her sandals were flat, her glasses oversized, and her bun loose. She hadn't bothered with make-up—just mascara and gloss—but she didn't care.

She. Didn't. Care. It was wonderful. And freeing.

The Abernathy clan stood in the centre of the garden, East Coast royalty. Jack had a blonde draped on his arm; Candice, his mum, wore natural pearls and snootiness, Jack's father, Edward, was brooding and unreadable. Jack's hand rested on his date's hip, and he held a glass of whiskey in his other hand. It was just gone noon, a bit early for hard liquor, but his drinking, thank God, wasn't her problem anymore.

She approached, sunglasses in hand, tapping them lightly against her thigh. Conversation around them began to slow as people turned and recognised her.

Candice's voice broke through first, pure ice. 'Calla. I don't believe you were invited.'

'I wasn't.' Calla shrugged, grateful she no longer had her as a mother-in-law. 'I gatecrashed. But as always, Candice, it all looks stunning. Elegant and ostentatious.'

Jack broke away from his companion, already bristling. 'If you're here to insult us, you can leave. Now. You're not part of this family anymore.'

'Something I thank God for,' she replied smoothly. 'But you can't blame me for thinking otherwise.'

Jack blinked. 'What's that supposed to mean?' he demanded.

She cocked her head. 'You've been asking me to come back. To return to Atelier Abernathy.'

'You're lying,' he spat, too fast, his eyes flicking nervously. 'I'd rather shove my face into hot coals.'

Calla lifted her phone. 'Really? Because I have messages. Lots of them. I'll read you some… Come back to AA. You know this is where you belong. You can't succeed on your own.' She read the next one slowly: 'I will keep sabotaging you until you return to me.'

Gasps rippled through the crowd.

'Jack's had trouble letting go,' Calla told the crowd, keeping her tone light. Her breathing was easier, her nerves gone. 'It's become…tiresome.'

Candice flushed purple. Jack's mouth opened, but no sound came out.

'And since we're being honest…' Calla continued, 'he was a pretty awful husband. He slept with my friends, our staff and our clients. He stole from our business and habitually humiliated me. I kept quiet out of shame. But not anymore.'

A murmur passed through the crowd—agreement? Disbelief? Their opinion didn't matter.

'He's also, frankly, a mediocre designer,' she added, shrugging as if it didn't hurt her. And it didn't. Jack's actions had no power over her anymore.

'Talking of designers who are subpar, how did you manage to land a commission like Sol House?' Jack demanded.

She tilted her head. 'You're about to accuse me of sleeping with Judah Reyes to get the commission, aren't you?'

His chin lifted, confirming her suspicions.

'I presume you sicced the paparazzi on us, right?' she said, sighing loudly. 'You're boring, Jack. So predictable and oh-so petty.'

'But you're still the slut who slept with her client!'

Knowing he'd lost the power to hurt her, Calla didn't flinch at his accusation. She was over letting him have any say in how she felt and what she did. She stepped in close, jabbing a finger into his chest. 'I am so done with you. With your sabotage, your lies, your tantrums. I want nothing to do with you or this family. Don't test me, Jack.'

He laughed, bitter and brittle. 'And how exactly do you plan to stop me?'

Calla was pretty sure Judah wouldn't mind her borrowing his clout. 'Oh, Jack…' She smiled. 'You seem to have forgotten who my "*client*" is. Judah Reyes, *the* Judah Reyes. If I ask, he'll put the word out and everyone will stop taking your calls.' She looked at Edward, then at Candice. '*All* of your calls.' She lifted an eyebrow. 'And you know that's not a bluff.'

Edward blanched. Candice looked like she might faint. Yeah, they understood the repercussions of going up against Judah.

'You can't come into our house and threaten—' Jack blustered.

'Jack, be quiet,' Candice snapped.

'I'm not going to just stand here—'

'Enough!' his father barked. He looked at Calla and nodded. 'This ends today. It will stop, Calla. You have my word.'

She held his gaze for a long, intense minute. 'Good.'

She turned to the crowd, who were still hanging on every word. This would be a party they remembered for all the wrong-for-the-Abernathys, right-for-her reasons. 'My apologies for the interruption. Enjoy your celebration. I'm Calla West, of Maison West.'

She walked away, shoulders straight, sunglasses back on, the guests buzzing behind her. She wouldn't look back.

She wasn't going in that direction anymore.

The sky was that impossible shade of island gold, a sunset so intense it made everything look like it had been kissed by honey and fire. Far out to sea, purple thunderclouds touched the ocean, the wind from the storm pushing the waves to crash over the rocks below.

Calla waited outside on Judah's vast outdoor area, sunglasses shielding her eyes. She hadn't wanted to knock on the front door like a visitor and didn't think she could walk into the house like it was hers. All she could do was wait. Calla slipped her foot out of her sandal and swished her toes through the pool's warm water. After Judah called her ten days ago, she'd spent the rest of the night thinking, and by morning, she knew what she had to do. Then, after she'd confronted the Abernathys, she'd given herself time for her new reality to settle, for the fears to calm down, to gather her courage.

Two weeks apart wasn't too long, right?

Calla heard the sliding door open, and she sucked in a long breath. But she still didn't run to him, waiting until he stepped out, barefoot, a beer in one hand. She recognised the exhaustion on his face.

He stilled at the sight of her, surprise flashing across his face before he buried it beneath his habitually implacable expression. She spoke before she lost her nerve. 'I'm not here for work or anything to do with work.'

Yet again, Judah's expression stayed neutral, but something flickered in his eyes—hope, maybe. She saw it, felt the pull of it. But she couldn't go there. Not yet.

'I'm here because I've got a few things to say.' She hauled in some air and brushed her fingers across her forehead, brushing a few strands of hair away. 'Will you listen?'

'Always.'

It was one simple word, but it gave her courage to continue. Judah gestured to the couches and waited for her to join him. After she sat down, he took the chair opposite her and rested his ankle on his knee. By not saying anything, he handed the moment over to her, and it was even more scary than she thought it would be.

'From the time I was young, I was Jack's wife, his family's daughter-in-law, the creative force behind their agency. After we divorced, I was the one who walked away, and everyone told me I wouldn't make it without them, and that I needed them to succeed.' She heard his growl of disagreement and appreciated it. 'That's not the case anymore.'

He heard something in her voice and tipped his head to the side. He narrowed his eyes. 'What did you do?' he asked.

It was a source of constant amazement that he, even after so little time, knew her so well.

'Well, the Abernathys always have a massive July Fourth gathering at their place in the Hamptons. It's one of the social events of the year.' Seeing his interest, and a hint of amusement on his face, a little of her tension dissipated. 'I gate-crashed it. And I caused a bit of a scene.'

'How big a scene?' he murmured, folding his arms. Was that a smidge of approval she heard in his voice?

She briefly described her confrontation with Jack and the back and forth between him and her.

Judah sat up straighter, his eyebrows lowering, and she knew he was angry. Calla held up her hand, silently asking him to settle down. 'I stood up for myself, told them, and everyone there, how Jack cheated on me, stole from me and that he's been hassling me to return to Atelier Abernathy.'

'Over my dead body.'

It wasn't, and would never be, an option. 'I also implied that he couldn't design himself out of a cereal box. Oh, and I borrowed you.'

'You did? How?'

'I hinted that the next time they swiped at me publicly, they'd better be prepared to take a financial beating because my lover was far richer and far more influential and would kill their businesses and source of income. Or words to that effect.'

'And he would, if that's what his lover asked him to do.'

Calla shook her head and placed her hand on her stomach, feeling the warmth deep inside her. 'The only thing they are truly scared of is having their good name tarnished and their business blackballed. I threatened both.'

'Good for you,' Judah quietly stated, his intense blue eyes not leaving her face. Calla knew what he was doing, and that he was waiting for her to come to him on her own terms.

And the beauty of it, the acceptance, made her want to cry.

'For ten years,' she said, voice low but steady, 'I tried to prove I belonged in their world, that I was good enough, for him and for them. Afterwards I wanted to prove them wrong, to prove that I wasn't weak. And that I wasn't their version of me, that I didn't need them to give me value.'

Judah's jaw ticked, but he still didn't speak.

Calla took a breath. 'But what I've really been doing is punishing myself. Jack never cared about me, he only cared that I had the balls to walk away from him without his permission, that I stepped away from him and his name. After him, I built a life with determination, steel and grit. But along the way, I forgot that you can't build anything real without softness too. I forgot, or was too scared, to let someone, anyone, in.'

She twisted her hands in her lap, fighting the urge to gnaw on her lip. 'Then I let you in, Judah. And I hated myself for it. Because I thought it made me weak and foolish. And worst of all, vulnerable.' Her chin lifted. 'But what I realised was that it made me brave.'

Judah finally exhaled. A long, slow breath. But he still didn't move. 'Calla...'

She shook her head, cutting him off gently. 'You don't need to say anything. I'm not even sure what comes next. I just—' Her voice broke. 'I just wanted to be the one who ran to you for once, the person who stays. I want to fight for the thing that made me feel alive again. And that's you.'

She made herself look at him, for their eyes to connect. 'But I might be too late. I really hope I'm not.'

'I told you I'd wait for you. I meant that,' he said quietly, his voice hoarser than before. Something fractured in his expression, then softened. 'I'm so glad you're here.'

He stood up, and with a quick shove of his bare foot pushed away the coffee table, and breeched the space between them. He hauled her up and into him. It felt like he'd been waiting to breathe deeply and then exhale, and now he finally could. Or maybe that was her.

Calla pressed her face to his chest, feeling his heartbeat steady and strong against her cheek.

For the first time in days, in weeks, maybe even years, she felt like she was where she belonged. But more than that? She felt whole.

Calla didn't know how long they stood there like that, wrapped around each other while the surf crashed and tumbled far below. Long enough for the heat of him to seep into her bones. Long enough for her pulse to slow and her heart to stop skittering like it was afraid of its own beat.

'I love you, Judah.'

'I love you, Cal. So much.' Judah pulled back just far enough to look at her. With a soft, full-of-wonder expression on his gorgeous face, he cradled her face like she was made of finely spun gold in danger of cracking. Infinitely rare and precious. 'I'm not going to lie, I had some sleepless nights wondering if I'd lost you. It was the longest two weeks of my life,' he said, voice rough with emotion.

'I'm sorry I made you wait,' Calla told him. 'And I'm glad you were still here at Sol House. That being said, I was prepared to go to London or back to New York to track you down. Even to Singapore.'

'I couldn't leave here without you,' he admitted.

Calla's throat tightened. 'Thank you for waiting for me.' Her voice trembled. 'I'm sorry I took so long, but I had to fight the urge to hide, to convince myself that, although I am too messy, too emotional, too much, I had to take a chance on you. On us.' She had to pull back, to loosen her hold. And yes, she was being insecure, but she needed to make sure…

'Can you tell me again? That you love me, that we are good?'

He closed his eyes for a beat and shook his head. 'Calla,' he said quietly, 'nothing has changed. I still love you. I will always love you. You are the only thing in my life that makes complete sense.'

She blinked, her heart stuttering. 'Really?'

'I've spent the best part of a year being who people needed me to be. The good heir. The golden boy son, the face of the brand. And it all felt so damn fake. Then you came back into my life—creative and brilliant and walking around pretending your heart didn't bleed—and you reminded me who I was.'

She shook her head. 'Judah…'

'You think you're the only one with wounds, that you're the one who's messy and messed up. But I've been hiding behind my fancy desk and title, behind the carefully curated social media posts uploaded by an intern in PR. My life looked great online, but until you came along, it felt like I wore a skin of sandpaper.'

His gaze pinned her feet to the floor. 'I needed to make some life changes, and so did you, sweetheart.'

She couldn't argue with that. Her eyes burned. 'It was tough without you, but I needed to do it by myself.'

'I know.' He grimaced. 'Walking away from you two weeks ago was so damn hard, but I didn't want to be one more person pushing you past your breaking point. I knew you had to walk this path alone. I just wasn't sure whether you would come back to me.'

A tear slipped down her cheek, and he caught it with his thumb. 'Can your end of the road be me, Calla? I'm yours if you want me,' he said, his voice fierce. She searched his face. Saw everything she'd been too afraid to believe: truth, acceptance, longing, desire—and his particular kind of love, deep and steady. Unquenchable.

'I'm scared,' she admitted.

'Me too,' he replied.

'But I don't want to run.'

He stepped closer. 'Then stay. Love me. Let me love you.'

'I do love you, and I am staying.' She rose onto her toes and kissed him. His hands found her waist, and hers curled around the back of his neck, and everything fell away. The fear, the past and the anxiety quieted.

They had no guarantees. No control.

But they had this moment. And more in the future. They were together. And this time, neither of them was letting go.

EPILOGUE

Six years later...

CALLA PUSHED HERSELF UP on the surfboard, wobbled, lost her balance and plummeted sideways, taking in a mouthful of seawater as a wave crashed over her head. Sighing, she used the seafloor to push herself to the surface and raked her hair back from her face.

Unlike her five-year-old son, Cody, who whizzed past her, expertly riding a wave on his smaller board, she was surfing challenged. She placed her hands on her hips and shook her head, proud of him and frustrated with herself. What was wrong with her? Why couldn't she do this?

'Don't give up your day job as Manhattan's most in-demand designer to become a professional surfer, sweetheart.'

Calla swivelled to look at her bare-chested husband, standing thigh deep in the sea, designer sunglasses on his face and their three-year-old daughter on his hip. Ivy held a conch shell in her hand and was inspecting it like it held all the secrets of the universe.

'You're really bad at surfing, but incredible at everything else,' he told her, his voice filled with love, that sexy smirk on his gorgeous face. Her heart stuttered; she was as much in love with Judah, no, more in love with him, than she'd ever been. Sexy, supportive and an utterly amazing dad, he was her world.

'Could it be that I have a terrible surfing instructor?' she mock demanded, hands on her hips.

'Dad, did you see me?' Cody yelled from the shore, his face alight with excitement. 'I did what you said, and I rode the wave to the shore!'

'You're amazing, bud,' Judah told him, his smile wide. He lifted his eyebrow at Calla, laughing. 'Our son doesn't think I'm so bad.'

Okay, maybe he was a decent instructor, and she was an awful surfer. That made more sense. Calla walked over to him, placed her hand on Ivy's chubby thigh and stood on her tiptoes to kiss the mouth that still made her insides clench and the space between her thighs heat. 'I will get up one day,' she told him, determination in her voice.

He nodded, curled his free arm around her waist, and hauled her closer to him. He kissed her wet head. 'I believe in you.'

It was a simple sentence, but it encapsulated so much about their relationship. Judah absolutely, fundamentally, from his head to the toes on his big feet, believed in her. When she took on her first major project after Sol House, and despite Judah spearheading Reyes Luxe's massive rebranding project, he'd listened to, encouraged and held her as she bombarded him with her thoughts, fears and worries.

When she spent three months suffering from morning sickness at the beginning of both her pregnancies, he fed her ginger crackers and sliced-up green apples, urging her to eat to combat the nausea. When she told him she wasn't strong enough to push their children into the world, that she was too exhausted, he kissed her forehead and reminded her that she was about to meet their son and daughter, and that she was already a marvellous mom. That she was all he needed, all he wanted…

Ivy tumbled from Judah's arms into hers, and they watched Cody lying flat on his board as he paddled over to him. When he reached them, Judah's mini-me sat astride his board and grinned at them. 'This is my favourite place in the world,' he informed them, his eyes sparkling.

In unison, she and Judah lifted their eyes to look at Sol House perched on the cliff high above them. The floor of the great room was covered in dinosaurs and dolls, cars and books. Pool toys littered the surface of their sexy infinity pool, and she was pretty certain Cody'd left a wet towel on a lounger. Earlier, Ivy had smooshed a biscuit into a cushion on the outdoor couch, and there was a good chance their new great dane puppy, Bandit, who'd they'd left to sleep, had chewed a flip-flop. Or two.

Their life, juggling parenthood and businesses, clients and the Reyes Luxe corporation, was full to overflowing, but Calla wouldn't swap it for anything, anywhere. Sol House and St Croix was her favourite home, and Judah, Cody, and Ivy were her everything.

She placed a kiss on Judah's tanned shoulder. 'Thank you for giving me this life,' she told him, her voice husky with emotion.

He covered his mouth with hers, lingering, feeding her his love. 'It is, as always, a joint effort, sweetheart. Thank you for walking out of that bar with me.'

She smiled and placed her hand on his rough-with-stubble cheek. 'Best decision ever.'

'Let's keep making those,' he murmured, pulling her closer, and Calla knew neither of them would ever let go.

* * * * *

If you enjoyed this story, check out these other great reads from Joss Wood

Fast-Track Dating Deception
The Tycoon's Diamond Demand
A Nine-Month Deal with Her Husband
Hired for the Billionaire's Secret Son

All available now!